S

H

I

SHIMMER

M

M

E

R

A JOHN METCALF BOOK

Shimmer

ALEX PUGSLEY

BIBLIOASIS
Windsor, Ontario

FIRST EDITION

10 9 8 7 6 5 4 3 2 1

Library and Archives Canada Cataloguing in Publication
Title: Shimmer / Alex Pugsley.
Names: Pugsley, Alex, 1963– author.
Description: Short stories.
Identifiers: Canadiana (print) 20210314516 | Canadiana (ebook) 20210314524 | ISBN 9781771964692 (softcover) | ISBN 9781771964708 (ebook)
Classification: LCC PS8631.U445 S55 2022 | DDC C813/.6—DC23

Edited by John Metcalf
Copyedited by Chandra Wohleber
Text and cover designed by Natalie Olsen

Portions of this work first appeared in the following publications: *Blood & Aphorisms, Acta Victoriana, Adelaide Literary Magazine, Canadian Notes & Queries, The Nashwaak Review, Spadina Literary Review, subTerrain,* and *Best Canadian Stories.*

This book was written with the support of the City of Toronto through the Toronto Arts Council. The author would also like to acknowledge funding support from the Ontario Arts Council, an agency of the Government of Ontario.

ONTARIO ARTS COUNCIL
CONSEIL DES ARTS DE L'ONTARIO
an Ontario government agency
un organisme du gouvernement de l'Ontario

ONTARIO CREATES | ONTARIO CRÉATIF

TORONTO ARTS COUNCIL | FUNDED BY THE CITY OF TORONTO

Canada Council for the Arts | Conseil des Arts du Canada

Canada

Published with the generous assistance of the Canada Council for the Arts, which last year invested $153 million to bring the arts to Canadians throughout the country, and the financial support of the Government of Canada. Biblioasis also acknowledges the support of the Ontario Arts Council (OAC), an agency of the Government of Ontario, which last year funded 1,709 individual artists and 1,078 organizations in 204 communities across Ontario, for a total of $52.1 million, and the contribution of the Government of Ontario through the Ontario Book Publishing Tax Credit and Ontario Creates.

PRINTED AND BOUND IN CANADA

To the kid with the Mohawk in the airport in Tucson

CONTENTS

S H I M M E R

Deedee at the 7-Eleven

"SO WHAT THE FUCK have you been *doing*, Veeper?" Wendell's voice is all loud and angry in the empty parking lot. "What the fuck, man? Where is it?"

I'm out on the highway and I lift my head up and look at Wendell in the distance there. It's Friday night and we always meet at the 7-Eleven but I guess I'm a little late. It's pretty dark but you can see Wendell because of the lights of the 7-Eleven store. Well you can't really see his face, but you can see his black baseball hat and his blond hair and his jacket's undone even though it's February.

"*Veeper?*"

Sometimes I feel like Wendell's been yelling at me like that for the last three years, ever since he gave me that nick-name in grade six. I kind of had this high-pitched voice back then. Wendell's a couple years older than me, he used to hang around my stepbrother, but we've been in the same grade ever since he failed some stuff in grade nine last year and I got put ahead. Actually me and Wendell got in a fight once when I first came to his school. I hit him in the cheek with a snowball in this big snowball fight. I just threw it, I didn't know where it was going, and I apologized and everything but he chased me for an hour saying he was going to get me. It was weird, because I could tell he was seeing if I was going to be afraid of him or not, and when he finally caught up with me he kind of went crazy and threw me down. We wrestled around in the snow and then I got on top of him and told him when I let him up I didn't want to fight anymore. But then when he got up, he just stood there throwing snowballs in my face saying, "You don't do that to Wendell Boudreau. You just don't *do* that to Wendell Boudreau" over and over. And I couldn't help it, I started crying and then everybody stayed there and I walked home by myself. That was the last time I ever cried in real life. I hated grade six.

So I'm out on the highway and I yell something back at Wendell and jump into these alders in the ditch. The alders are all covered in ice and start clicking each other as I'm walking through them. I drink what's left in one of my beers. I've had two or three beers by now that I got from my mother's and so things are starting to kind of swirl by me. I toss the empty bottle so it'll roll across the ground without breaking. I always do that. I like that thing where you just stop and watch the bottle spin over the frozen ground, over the ice that's frozen in old footprints.

Because then it's like only some weird coincidence that you're seeing it.

"So Veeper," Wendell says, looking at me, "did you get the two-four or what? What's going on?"

We talk in this girl's voice sometimes and I start talking in it. "Okay don't say hi. Don't say hi, you snob. You two-faced snob."

"So what's going on? Fuck, man. What are you saying? I want to get going."

"I guess I'm saying I couldn't get in."

"Oh, *man*," Wendell says, shaking his head. "I don't fucking believe it. Are you serious?"

"Of course I'm serious," I go. "I'm totally fucking serious. I-couldn't-get-in. What's your problem?"

"Oh and that's great. That is just fucking great."

"Excuse me for living. You got a hot date lined up or something?" There's one of those big garbage dumpsters in the middle of the parking lot and I start flicking stuff from my pockets into it. Cigarette wrappers, receipts, old candy. "Take it easy," I say. "I got Donny to go in for us. He's bringing it in the Nova." Then I crack up like I can't help it.

Wendell doesn't say anything. He's watching one of the cigarette wrappers blow off in the wind. "You fucking *hope* Donny's bringing it in the Nova," he goes. He turns around and puts a knuckle to the side of his nose and blows something out of it. Then he wipes his nose with the sleeve of his jacket and spits. Wendell can spit about four different ways. He's got a chink in his front tooth he can spit out of and he can also make these little spit bubbles under his tongue and send them floating down streets or football fields or parking lots or whatever.

He sniffs something in his nose and looks at me. "Aren't you just Mr. Fucking Comedian tonight," he goes.

"Yeah well whatever. Some friend *you* are." I stomp the snow off my boots on the pavement and pass Wendell one of the beers I got left. Then I pull a last beer out of my pocket and lean against the side of the steps. "Fucking cold," I say, seeing the bottoms of my jeans are frozen. "Fucking nine-point-four freeze-your-bag-off. It's cold. I'm cold."

"You weren't waiting outside since seven-thirty."

"So whyn't you wait inside the 7-Eleven?"

"Fucking chinks kicked me out."

"No way! They kicked you out? That is great." I start laughing. Me and Wendell are always laughing at stuff no one else thinks is funny.

I don't know why Wendell's been here since seven-thirty. I guess I don't know where he's living these days. His dad moved to Florida and his mother's got like a split-personality thing and Wendell can't stand living with her anymore so maybe he's crashing at his cousin's place. I don't know where he's coming from.

"So," I go, "I seen Eddie Fong and some of those grade tens at the liquor store."

"Oh yeah?" Wendell chugs the beer I gave him and tosses the bottle into the garbage can beside the steps. "They get in?"

"I guess they did. Eddie did. He's got that – you know that moustache he's got now? He doesn't look like too much of a goof, no. He's pretty funny. He was saying his dog found his hash and ate it and it's been walking around in a body-stone for a week."

"Yeah?" Wendell goes, cracking a huge burp. He talks in this burp-voice sometimes. "What're those guys doing tonight?"

"They were talking about going down to Deedee's after."

"Deedee's?" Wendell goes, looking at me like I just told him to fuck off. "I don't think so, Veeper. I don't fucking think so." He turns to the wall of the 7-Eleven and starts kicking at some icicles. "Fucking snow in my boot."

"Don't lace them up whatever you do."

Wendell doesn't say anything for a second. He just burps again. "I fucking doubt that about them going to Deedee's, Veeper. I don't think so."

I shrug like I could care less and look out at the highway. It's starting to snow again. Little snowflakes spin out of the dark, whizzing around the lights of the 7-Eleven and around the street lights at the intersection with Highway Seven. If you squint at the lights they get little halos around them from the snow.

Wendell takes off his hat and shakes his hair out. "Jesus fuck, you know, Veeper, I wanted to start drinking *now*, right? Fuck, man. And you know Eddie Fong? He's a fucking druggie, isn't he?"

I shrug and don't say anything. The snowflakes were

kind of making me remember something. I was thinking all kinds of stuff. I remember this one night at this Valentine's dance in grade eight. Deedee, she was smiling, she was really drunk and everything, looking at me, trying to lick my hand and get the stamp off it to get into this dance. It was snowing and the sky was pink even though it was around twelve o'clock at night. After the dance I walked her home in the snow and we went and sat in the visitors dugout at this Little League baseball diamond and we made out and I sort of felt her up but it was embarrassing because she was really drunk and didn't even know her hair was in her mouth and then I thought she was going to puke. That was the second time I ever kissed her actually because we made out in a closet at Tanya Chisholm's birthday party in grade five. And she wrote me this letter once from the principal's office on the inside-out part of a pack of cigarettes that I still got somewhere. I put it in an old Dennis the Menace comic, I think. Actually now I can't remember where I put it. I might've lost it when we moved.

"And is he going to Deedee's, you think?" Wendell's saying.

"Who's this?"

"Eddie Fong!"

"Well, I imagine. What the fuck did I just get through saying?"

Wendell looks at me really weird for a second, then shakes his head like he's shaking something out of it.

"Aw, fuck," he says. "Fuck it. If that's the way it's going to be, then just fuck it, right? Fuck Deedee and fuck her party."

"Why? What's going on? What are you talking about?"

"I'm serious, Veeper," Wendell goes, pulling his hat back on. "Don't fuck around, man. Don't fuck me around."

"Eddie Fong's just a *guy*. He's just a fucking guy."

"Yeah? I heard he was a fucking idiot. I heard he was a fucking dick."

"Oh for fuck's sakes," I go. "I don't know what you're talking about then. I don't know." I start laughing. I kind of make myself start laughing at how *serious* we just got and I look around the parking lot like maybe I dropped something in it. I watch my breath for a second then look over at Wendell's hat. "You going after someone else? You and Deedee still going out?"

"I don't know," Wendell goes. He's sort of kicking at the new snow on the pavement. "That girl, she's fucked. Fucked in the head. I'm serious."

"Why's that?"

"Oh my fuck, Veeper. It's different now. It's really different. You wouldn't fucking believe it."

"Believe what?"

"Oh man, I don't know. It's a fuck-up. It's fucked up."

"No."

"Oh *yes*," Wendell goes, looking around like there's someone else with us. "Like the other night, all right? A bunch of us are drinking in the park behind the school, right? Okay, so Deedee, she comes down and gets there and all of a sudden it's like she's really pissed *off* at me and everything, you know. Wanting to *know* everything. As if she's Little Miss Innocent and hasn't ever done anything to piss *me* off. Her and Sheri both of them. Fucking all this shit, saying that I never –" Wendell closes his eyes a second. "Oh Veeper, man, they just try and turn everything into some big fuck-up relationship talk, you know? Every time. And I don't fucking need it, right? I just don't fucking need it. I mean, you know, it's not like I don't like Deedee. I like Deedee. I *like* Deedee. But I just don't need any of that fucked-up shit, you know. I don't fucking need it and I fucking hate it. I *hate* it."

I've been staring at Wendell but now I don't know where to look so I just look at those little halos around the street lights. But I can't really see them anymore. I try and think of something to say and then I just start yawning instead.

"I think we're going to have to do some real serious drinking tonight," Wendell is saying, spitting into the new snow. "We might have to get really fucking shit-faced tonight."

I shrug or something but I feel like there's a couple other things I can't remember. I don't know if I'm drunk or what. "You got any smokes?"

Wendell doesn't say anything. He's working his mouth so he can spit one of his bubbles into the air.

"You want anything in the store?"

He shakes his head.

I put my beer on the ground and go up the steps. In the reflection in the glass door I can see Wendell looking at the little spit bubble he just put into the wind. It's floating over somebody's car, up toward one of the lights.

WHEN I COME BACK OUT, I want to say something to Wendell about Deedee's party and Eddie Fong and Sheri and all that when I see two girls coming over the pile of snow at the end of the parking lot. One of the girls is Sheri and for a second I think the other one's Deedee – she has hair like Deedee – but then I see it's no one I really know.

"Well, look who it is," I go. "Two little piggy-wigs come to market."

"Hey!" Sheri calls out, grabbing at the other girl as she's sliding down the snowbank. "Look who's at the 7-Eleven."

"It's Veeper," the other one goes. "Hey, gorgeous."

"So guys," Sheri yells. "Going to any parties tonight?"

"Maybe," Wendell goes, slumping back against the wall. "Where you going?"

The girls walk toward us all stooped over and pigeon-toed. For a second I think they're going to see that beer bottle I threw down over there and I don't know why but I don't want them to see it. I just don't want them to see it. Sheri's got something watery hanging off the end of her nose and her hair looks sort of frozen, like she left the house with it wet. She's got this really big nose, too. She didn't really have one when she was a kid but she started to get one around grade seven. She always knows who everyone's going out with but I don't think she's gone out with anyone personally since at least two summers ago when she went out with a guy at some music camp. Actually I heard once she and Wendell got together after a Halloween dance, but then they both pretended like it never happened.

The other girl I don't know. She's stumbling around, leaning into Sheri. She starts laughing at something and then she's sucking on her cigarette and trying to blow smoke rings and bubbles with her gum at the same time.

"Where we going?" Sheri says, staring at Wendell like she's got some terrific secret. "Wouldn't you like to know? So Wendell, you seen Deedee lately?"

"No," Wendell says, talking in his burp-voice, "haven't seen her."

"Well, maybe because she's with somebody else tonight maybe."

"So?"

"So maybe she's with Eddie Fong."

"So?" Wendell goes, burping again.

"*So?*" Sheri says, looking at me. "So what! So long for you, Wendell-baby." Then Sheri drops her head back and starts cracking up like it's the funniest thing she's ever heard.

It's really snowing now. Instead of blowing away, the snowflakes start sticking to the first thing they hit. There's snow in the girls' hair and on Wendell's hat and I can feel it sticking in my eyelashes.

Sheri's friend is trying to stand up straight. When she sees me she kind of puts her lips together and gives me this special look. She's wearing a lot of eye makeup and her parka and her shirts and everything are all undone pretty far down so you can kind of see this light blue lacy bra peeking out from underneath. She has very big tits or breasts or whatever and I don't want her to think I'm some peeping Tom but I keep looking back at her and whenever I do I feel bad because this girl is trying to look me right in the eye. It makes me feel weird. Her looking at me with that bra and everything gives me this really weird feeling in my ass.

"Well," I go, "Mr. Storekeeper is all out of du Maurier."

"I got du Maurier, Veeper," Sheri goes, coming over to me. You can smell liquor on her breath. Lemon gin. Panty-remover's what Donny calls it. Sheri shakes a mitten off her hand and starts looking inside her coat. "Here you go, babe," she goes, handing me a crumpled-up du Maurier Special Mild. Then she starts leaning on my shoulder so she can pull her sneaker back on her foot. It kind of takes me by surprise because I was putting her cigarette behind my ear. I don't smoke Special Milds.

"It's my last one," Sheri goes. "But you can have it. You can have it. You know, you're looking good these days, Veep. I think you're looking real good. Ain't he, Celeste? He's cute."

"He's sweet," the other girl goes, staring at me. Then she bends over and kind of throws her head back, swinging her hair away from her face. When her hair settles back down she takes this deep breath and starts tucking in all her shirts.

"So," Wendell says, putting his hands behind his head, "everybody's going to Deedee's then? That the plan?"

"Thought you didn't care," Sheri goes. She looks at me like she's going to say something, then turns and faces Wendell. "The way you treat her like shit she should've dropped you ages ago."

"Yeah, you watch your mouth, Sheri," Wendell goes. "You fuck around, girl."

"Oh I fuck around, do I?" Sheri says. "Well *you're* the one who fucks around, Wendell Boudreau. And you can just fuck yourself from now on, boy. Jesus, are you fucked up or what? I can't believe it. I know you. You always got to act so fucking *different* around people, don't you? You always got to fucking ignore everybody. What's going on with you anyway? Deedee went on the *pill* for you, you fucking prick, you ignorant fucking prick! Christ!"

Sheri's starting to cry now. She hitches up her pants and wipes at her nose. "Oh my God, Veeper," she says. "I can't understand why you'd even hang around him. It's pathetic, I swear to God. And you know, Deedee, she always used to tell me how much she liked you anyway. Aw, fuck. I don't know what's going on with you guys anymore and I don't fucking care either. You can just go to hell for all I care. You're the same – conceited fucking bastards. You're just out for what you can get. Come on, Celeste. We're going. I wouldn't waste my time."

I'm shivering now as I watch Celeste follow Sheri out of the parking lot. There's the sound of breaking glass and Sheri laughing, then they're gone.

I feel kind of bad about not looking at that Celeste girl, for not looking her in the eye. I feel bad about it.

"So spare me this shit," Wendell goes, shaking his head like he can't believe any of this. "Fuck that noise." He kicks around in the new snow and stubs his boot on a big chunk of ice underneath. "*Slut!*" Wendell screams, kicking at the chunk till it breaks away. He picks it up in his bare fingers and heaves it at the dumpster. It crashes to the pavement halfway, sending bits of ice and snow everywhere. "Okay," Wendell goes, wiping his hands on his jeans. He's smiling now like everything's a big joke. "How fucking fascinating, right? Okay. So Veeper. What do you want to do? What do you want to do, man? You want to go to this party or what?"

I'm feeling kind of distracted thinking about Sheri and that Celeste girl and then I remember I still got Sheri's cigarette behind my ear. I go to flick it away or put it in my pocket but I don't know what to do with it so I'm just kind of spacing out looking at it. For a second I'm thinking I'd like to see it in one of those spinning beer bottles.

"Look Veeper," Wendell goes, "we're getting really drunk tonight, all right? We're getting *wasted*, man. You up for it or what? Come on. Come on, *Veep*."

Something in Wendell's voice is really pissing me off and I have to keep looking down at the cigarette because I feel like I'm kind of freaking out. My face feels like it's two hundred degrees. I go to say something when Donny's Nova comes honking and sliding into the parking lot.

Wendell yells "Thank fucking God" and runs over to get in the front seat.

I'm still standing there holding that stupid, crumpled-up du Maurier Special Mild that no one's ever going to smoke. I was kind of tapping it against my lips. I didn't know what I was thinking. I didn't know if I wanted to keep drinking or go to Deedee's or what. I knew I wanted to get the fuck away from the 7-Eleven but I didn't really feel like seeing Sheri or that Celeste girl again. I didn't even feel like seeing Deedee. I took the cigarette away from my mouth to look at it and right then I had this thing where I knew everything was going to get a lot weirder from now on.

Before the After-Party

"SO ARE YOU COMING, sweetpea?" Mia spoke into her flip phone. "Where *are* you guys?" She held her free hand over her other ear, a red Michael Kors purse dangling from the crook of her elbow. She wore a black shift dress – short-sleeved with a flounce trim – and with her clear complexion and sharp cheekbones she was, even by the standards of her industry, rather instantaneously noticeable. "At the Nada show? Still? That's wack. You should be here. Come to the address I texted! Don't you want something to happen?" Mia touched at a cowlick that sprang against the sweep of her bangs. "What*ever,* bitch. Because you're coming." She listened. "I recognize that. I get it. But you should totally come. Oh my fucking *God,* yes. Just come already. You can definitely, absolutely, no problem get in. I'm not even kidding. I put your names on the door so let the night begin, freak. Text me when you get here!" She snapped shut her flip phone and whirled around. "My friends are being doinks –" she started to say but found to her slight surprise that she was alone in the condo.

She had only a moment to take in her surroundings – open concept, parquet flooring, leather sofa, balcony – before she heard her name called in the outside hallway. Keeping her head down a little, for she'd learned to be judicious about eye contact, she smiled in the direction of the open front door where Steve, the condo's owner, was just now appearing.

Steve wore a Canali suit, carried a gift bag, and walked with some swiftness. There was something about this swiftness which seemed an extension of his confidence, prospects, and sense of purpose.

"So," Steve said, moving to the marble-topped kitchen island, "you talk to your pals?"

"Yep." Mia slipped a hand under her dress to scratch at her collarbone. "But they're being idiots. Because here's the deal –"

"There's a deal?"

"They've gotten into the absolute dumbest habit, it's just actual garbage, really, of total procrastination so they don't even know if they're coming now."

"Ah," he said, "that is definitely a deal." He dropped the gift bag on the kitchen island. "You forgot your swag bag in the elevator. I didn't know if you wanted it or not."

"Cool," she said, reaching for it, "let's see the swag." She pulled out a bottle of Naya natural spring water, a MAC matte lipstick, an issue of *Elle Canada*, L'Oréal EverCreme Deep Nourish shampoo, several individually wrapped Guylian chocolates, a gift certificate for a free laser eye surgery consultation, as well as a psychedelic flyer for a future event.

Looking at the flyer, Mia read aloud the event's name. "'Tits and Glitz'?" She waggled it above her head. "Tacky much?"

"My company's sponsoring that."

"Sounds like a porn show."

"It's a fundraiser."

"For tits?"

"For breast cancer."

"Oh," said Mia, fingering at her cowlick, as if suddenly concerned it should curve to the left. "I think I remember this. Didn't someone's sister die of breast cancer or something?"

Steve was about to reply when a female commotion began out in the hallway. "So who do we have to fuck to get a drink around here?" asked a woman's voice.

Through the door came a full-figured woman – Twyla – and with her perfectly layered bob, sheer camisole, and embroidered bra, she might have been the host of a makeover series, or the lead buyer for a big-box store, or the editor of an in-flight magazine.

Some steps behind her was Gary, a short man with wavy blond hair whose multi-purpose smile showed he felt at ease anywhere.

"Hey," said Gary, "have you guys played the 'Friends' drinking game?"

"Have I played the 'Friends' drinking game?" said Twyla. "No, I have my own drinking game. It's called 'Being Twyla.'"

"Twyla –" Steve clapped his hands and smiled, as if delighted to be welcoming more guests. "What can I get you? Vodka tonic? Grey Goose? Gary, that work for you?"

"I'm just glad," said Gary, moving toward the balcony to look at the ten-storey view, "you don't live in Parkdale. I don't need to see some bag lady randomly having a crap on the sidewalk. Who wants to see that?"

"Totally." Steve poured vodka shots into four highball glasses. "If I want to see a bag lady taking a crap, I want it planned, I want it organized, I want an itinerary."

"Ha!" Twyla watched Steve drop a lemon slice into each drink. "I *like* him. What's his name again? Is it Dave?"

"Me?"

"Aren't you supposed to be my cabana boy?"

"Steve," said Steve, coming over to shake her hand.

"Right. Steve. Little tip? You're gay. Feel that handshake? You're a gay-boy. Put that in your BlackBerry. 'Really cute but I'm gay.' You just haven't come out yet. But you will. You will. It's still possible. Anything's possible." She turned to Mia. "And who do we have here?"

"That's Mia," said Gary, coming over to grab a vodka tonic. "Mia the model."

"Well," said Twyla, regarding her, "you're your own

kind of perfect, aren't you? I love that your lipstick matches your purse but, seriously, you're too gorgeous. I can't look at you. It's making me sick. And how *old* are you? Because you look twelve. Have you even had sex yet? How many times, though? Because you look like you've had sex with two partners, tops. You know what I mean, Stevie-boy? She's so *dewy*." Frowning, Twyla picked up one of the vodka tonics. "And I know I should get around to having my first lesbian experience, it's on my to-do for sure, but I'm too chicken. Every time I think of a woman down in my punani?" She shivered. "*Ew*. Why is that, Steve? Can we discuss this? I have issues, obviously."

"You and me both, Twyla," said Steve, passing a vodka tonic to Mia. Steve raised his glass and said, "Here's to the night!"

"Bottoms up."

"Cheers, people!"

"Whatever."

"So, Mia," said Gary, "this your first Fashion Week? Doing a lot of shows?"

"Not really." Mia shrugged. "It's so exorbitant now. This year's crazy. The busiest ever. And normally I wouldn't do Fashion Week because everyone will want to know why I'm quitting modelling –"

"Quitting?" repeated Twyla, as she sat on the leather sofa.

"Well," said Mia, briefly glancing at Steve, "I think you really have to want it. And I'm not sure I do. There's so much other stuff in life besides running around to go-sees, drinking Red Bull, and getting your hair pulled out by stylists, you know? Like, I'll do Milan then that's it."

"Good for you," said Gary.

"What about you?" Mia asked him.

"I don't think –" Gary waited to finish a yawn. "Anyone wants to see me on a runway."

"I mean, what do you do?"

"What do I do? In marketing?"

"Sure. What's that all about?" Mia checked the time on her flip phone. "I'm here to learn."

"Well –" Gary shrugged. "Depends what you're looking for. I'd say most of the time it's about expressing the brand story. Optimizing the message. But" – he looked at each of them – "the advertising industry's in flux right now. Selling the Coors Light account, that used to be a no-brainer. That was throwing Maxim chicks at the consumer, pitching a nineties ideal, and playing Oasis in the background." Gary drank from his vodka tonic. "But that's not going to work anymore. Not in 2008. Not to an eighteen-year-old. Because he's going to say, 'You can't market to me. I download my music and ring tones and watch movies on my iPhone. I've created my bundle.'" A spiel-friendly tone had arrived in Gary's voice, as if he were giving a presentation at a media conference. "We live in a bundle society now. Phone. Cable. Banking. Are there still opportunities? Absolutely. Ten years from now, this is going to be one big borderless planet and the challenge's going to be how to build solutions that really kick it up a few floors to make a connection. It's about making a connection."

"I'm not here to judge," said Twyla, gazing at Gary with profound annoyance, "but what the fuck are you blabbering about? I mean, yes, Gary, I feel your presence and you're choosing this moment to wow us with your badassery. I get it. But, dude, are you kidding me?" She stood up. "Because what's your playlist? Fifty minutes of commercial-free good time, great oldies for the drive home? Because if you're going to pose as some sort of advertising guru, get your shit straight, big talker. Number one, it's not going to be about consumers getting an identity from the brands they purchase. It's going to be about making the consumers the brand. Number two, it's not about marketing at them. It's going to be about listening *to* them because it's going to be about coordinating your content with how they see the world. So you may want to get on that train and off the dickhead express."

"Is it that time already?" asked Gary. "Steve? Mia? A pleasure." He plunked his unfinished vodka tonic on the kitchen island. "Twyla? All the best with the twelve steps. I'm done." He walked out into the hallway, not bothering to close the front door.

Following a moment of disquiet, Mia exchanged a glance with Steve.

"What?" said Twyla, noticing this interaction. "You think I should apologize? Look, Gary's a good time. No, no.

He is. Don't get me wrong. It's just I can't deal with the whole Gary situation right now." She scowled. "Because he comes in with his tan and his floofy hair and his GQ weirdness and I *know* he owns his own marketing firm but his haircut is douchey therefore his argument's invalid." Downing her vodka tonic, she turned to Mia. "Look, I'll just say it. Gary's got a small-man complex in a big way. And I find it creepy when short men are horny. Am I right, Mia? It's like a hobbit with no pants running around with a little chubby no one knows what to do with." Facing Steve, she said, "And I'm sorry if I ruined your party, handsome, but guys like Gary, they just *so* drain my battery. I mean, I'm trying to put some realness into the proceedings but if y'all think I went too far I'll go and apologize. Jesus." She set her empty glass on the kitchen island.

Steve and Mia both stared at this empty glass, as if briefly mesmerized.

"But one thing," said Twyla, "if I can leave you with one thing." She walked up to Steve and placed her hand on the smoothness of his cheek. "There's a whole other world out there, Steven."

"Uh-huh?" he said. "A secret world behind everything I see?"

"Just waiting for you to find it." She play-slapped his face. "Keep your phones on, kids. See you on the rooftop."

Mia watched Twyla stroll out the front door, then spun to Steve with a look of wonder. "What the fuck?"

"Well," said Steve, "that was magical, wasn't it?"

"Holy diatribe," said Mia, "she gets so doodled up! But I don't know if she really pertains to what Gary was doing, exactly, you know?"

"I think I agree."

"Oh well" – Mia shrugged, palms upturned – "people are human."

"Some are. How are you for drinks, Mia?"

"Maybe some water?" She moved to the kitchen island and snatched the bottle of Naya natural spring water. "I only had a little bump but I am geeking out. Don't worry. It's just something my brain does." She twisted the cap off the spring water. "So the after-party's on your own building's rooftop? How cool is that?"

"Oh," said Steve, "that space is used for a lot of parties."

"Do you actually *own* this condo?"

"I do," said Steve. "I'm in Toronto so much I thought I'd get a place."

"Really? How old are you?"

"Thirty-one."

"For real?" She held up a baby finger. "Pinky swear?"

"Pinky swear," he said, touching his baby finger to hers. "Thirty-one."

"You look younger."

"Kiehl's."

"Mmm," said Mia, "you know your brands, I have to say. So what were you doing ten years ago? When you were my age?"

"Ten years ago I was in a dorm in Ithaca, throwing pizza at my best friend, and trying to read 'The Wealth of Nations.'"

"And now you have this condo? I should read that book."

"Then that friend and I started a video game company. And now I'm on the road twenty-three days out of every month. Tomorrow I'm in Philadelphia. Then Syracuse and Rochester. Tuesday and Wednesday it's Detroit and Chicago."

"So what do you do there?"

"Check in with the sales reps. Half of my life is getting bombed with the sales reps. And there's a lot of sales reps." Steve seemed to be staring at Twyla's empty glass. "I mean, the travel's not all bad. Some cities are fine. Except Boston. If I could live my life over, I'd never go to Logan Airport." He put the empty glass in the sink. "But wherever I am, every time I wake up, it's the same thing. Bedside table. Television. Curtains. No clue where I am. I know everybody has that nightmare but I wake up four times a week like that." He went to the freezer and took out another bottle of Grey Goose. "And relationships? When's that going to happen? My college friends tried setting me up. They don't bother anymore. Women can't relate to me. They hear I'm a CEO and that's all they see. I mean I could probably date all kinds of people. But the truth is, most of the time I'd just as soon watch the porn channel in the hotel room. Less complicated." He took out a clean highball glass. "My life's kind of fucked, really. Do I do anything normal? Play on a squash ladder? Have a barbecue? Coach Little League? When's that going to happen? Look, I've got friends in twelve different cities and I can find something to do every night. But the people I see, the friends I have, it's all sort of situational. 'Making a connection?' Tell me about it. Basically someone's your friend if you can do something for them. *Then* they're your friend. It's gross that it's true. But it's true." He poured a shot of vodka into the glass and added tonic and a lemon slice. "That's why Gary's the way he is. He's got to buy all the drinks. He's got to tell the dumbest jokes. He's got to sound like he understands all the trends and start-ups from every point of view. I've met a hundred Garys. He's in every city. At every conference. In every bar. And he's not even a haircut. He's barely a meme." Steve looked into his vodka tonic. "But, fuck, maybe I'm no better. Talk to me in ten years when I've turned into another high-performance dipshit. Talk to me when I've turned into Gary." Sipping his drink, he looked over at Mia. "How did I get on that track? *My* little diatribe? Probably the coke talking."

"No," Mia said emphatically, "I liked it."

"You did?"

"Because it's real. Because you're talking about something that matters to you. Even if it's weird or personal at least it's honest. Because here's the thing" – she made a series of quickly distinctive gestures, as if guiding a particularly wayward aircraft onto a runway – "if you never said anything for real then seriously you *would* be Gary."

Although she spoke these last words with a throwaway intonation, her voice was inflected with a thoughtfulness Steve hadn't registered before. But he was registering it now. In fact, he was looking at her with real interest when a musical signal sounded on her flip phone.

"Opa!" said Mia. "That's probably my pals." She read a text. "Yup. They're on the rooftop. Let me just text them back."

As Mia sat on the sofa, two-thumbing a reply, Steve stared at her. In the glow of the flip phone's screen, her face – dark eyes, upturned nose, pouting lips – appeared so beautiful that Steve, moved by the moment, took a spontaneous step forward and touched at the bounce of her cowlick.

"The fuck?" Mia sprang up from the sofa. "So, um, I should really go see my friends." She snapped her thumb and fingers together in hurried farewell. "So, yeah, bye!"

Without another look, she strode out the front door, head up, shoulders back, her purse swinging into and knocking a Burberry umbrella off the door handle.

LEFT ALONE, Steve moved to the stainless-steel refrigerator, not caring about the fallen umbrella, not bothering to close the front door. From the freezer, he took a pack of American Spirit cigarettes and a yellow Bic lighter. He walked toward the balcony and unlocked the glass sliding door. Pushing it open, he stepped onto the balcony.

He sat in one of two cedar Adirondack chairs, recent purchases still in store plastic, and rested his shoes on an empty clay flowerpot. He lit a cigarette, setting the cigarette pack and the lighter on the chair arm, and then looked out at the city.

A shrill noise – the persistent beeping of a commercial vehicle in reverse – began on the street below. Without really knowing what it was, Steve listened to it for a full half minute, then he looked up and watched the distant lights of an airplane as it travelled across the sky. Of course it had been his own sister who had died from breast cancer – three years ago last Christmas – and mostly he was able to keep in check his feelings of loss. But there were some moments when, taken with the events of a day, or the mistakes of a night, he felt susceptible to strange infinities, as he did now, on this damp night in March, alone on a balcony in Toronto.

THERE WERE sharp footsteps on the parquet floor inside, the scud and clack of high heels, and Steve was twisting to see who it was when Mia materialized on the balcony.

"Hey," she said, shyly waving her open flip phone above her head, "someone would like to talk to you."

Looking a trifle amazed, both by Mia's return and by this impending conversation, Steve took the flip phone and placed it on the chair arm. "Hey," he said, pressing the speakerphone button.

"Sweet Baby Jesus –" From the phone crackled Twyla's voice and, after a few bumpy seconds of fallout, this voice resumed, somewhat obscured by ambient chatter. "Steve? You there?"

"Twyla," said Steve, "I've been worried. What's up?"

"Steve! It's the after-party for real. Are you kidding me? There's like a fafillion fairy lights on the rooftop. And a canopy. And balloons. People are having sex with balloons."

"Sweet."

"This shit is *happening*, Steven. Can you take it? Can you handle it? Is it real? But here's a question. What are you doing right now?"

"Me?" Steve watched Mia take one of his cigarettes, neatly cup her hands together, and light it with his lighter. "Why do you ask?"

"Because I love you, cowboy. Can I just say that? And tell Mia she was the most beautiful at the show tonight. Everyone noticed her. You did, for sure. But your friend's kind of a creeper."

"Who? Gary?"

"He's fucking hammered and hitting on everybody. No, no, seriously, he is on his way to oblivion. He's lost. *So* lost. It's over. It's done. I'm deleting him out of my phone. But let's get back to you –"

"Finally."

"Because, Stevie, you're like me. Tired of the scene. Tired of all the random hookups. I mean, we've fucked a lot of people but have we ever really made love? Keep that visual. Try that on for size. Take back the night, Steve-O. Everybody poops. But, seriously, are you still there?"

"Barely." He watched Mia exhale a perfect plume of smoke. "I'm barely holding on."

"Because you got to let me in! How can I feel your pain if you won't let me work my magic?"

"There's magic?"

"Yes! Just experience it for once. For once in your fucked-up Courtney Love life, Steven. Come to the rooftop. Just think what can happen. It'll be amazing."

"As wonderful as that sounds, Twyla –"

"Oh, don't tell me you're going to punk it! Steve-A-Reeno, you used to be so much fun. What happened there? You're jaded. So jaded. Why don't you come up and have a little drinkie? I'll make it worth your while, believe –"

"Night, Twyla!" interrupted Mia, leaning over the phone. "Talk later." She flicked away a spark from the bust-line of her dress and snapped the phone shut. Then, rather as if they were in the habit of sharing cigarettes, she offered the rest of her cigarette to Steve.

"I didn't know you smoked," said Steve, taking it.

"All my training as a model." Mia tilted her head. "That Twyla, she can be pretty superfluous."

"Yes." Steve dragged on the cigarette and dropped the still-burning stub into the empty flowerpot. "Yes, she can." He stood up. "Shall we go in?"

Inside, he closed the front door and walked to the kitchen island. Mia's gift bag had fallen on its side, its contents haphazard on the marble-topped counter. Picking up the "Tits and Glitz" flyer, he stuck it absently to the refrigerator with a circular black magnet.

Mia sat on the leather sofa, watching him. "I'm sorry if I was a jerk before," she said, "when I asked about that fundraiser."

"Oh," said Steve, "what was your phrase? People are human? And, look, sorry if *I* was a jerk before when I got in your personal space."

"Hmm," she said reflectively, smoothing her eyebrow with a fingertip. "Hey, is there any more Grey Goose?" She slipped out of her high heels and tucked her bare feet under her thigh. "Maybe I could have a teensy-weensy vodka tonic?"

"I don't see why not."

He was pouring vodka into a fresh highball glass when her flip phone rang.

Mia took it out of her purse, glanced at the call display, and let it ring.

"Mia?"

"Hmm?"

He held up the glass to show a half ounce of vodka. "That look right?"

"Perfect."

He added the tonic, lemon slice, and ice cubes and brought the drink to her.

"Steve?" said Mia, taking a quick sip and placing the drink on the floor. "Can I ask you a question?"

Spotting a fallen chocolate on the floor, Steve knelt down to pick it up. "Of course."

"And if I do, will you promise to tell the truth?"

"Always." Still on one knee, he held up his baby finger. "Pinky swear."

Hooking her baby finger in his, Mia swung it twice and released it. "If I hang here tonight, in a sleepover kind of situation" – she gazed into his eyes and then, untucking a foot, pushed two toes against his chest – "can we do something you've never done before?"

"What do you mean?" asked Steve, as if baffled, "like skydiving?"

"Yeah," said Mia, pulling the flounce trim of her dress to her waist, "like skydiving."

Mia remained on the sofa for some time, holding Steve's head with both hands, pulling him closer, her dilated eyes flashing from the ceiling to the fallen umbrella to the flyer stuck to the refrigerator. The flyer was still there some months later, for Mia would remember seeing it, in all its psychedelia, and half wondering what it was, when she returned from doing the Lancôme campaign in New York, long after she'd moved in.

Legion

BUT WHAT TIME'S IT? What time's it, boys? We got enough time for another round or what? It's later now than it's ever been, eh? How's she going, Merna? Be good enough to bring us a tray of draft over here, would you, sweetheart? Hello, Merna! I say could you bring us some more beer, please. We're just getting started over here, isn't that right, boys? And Merna, you going to show us your tits later or what? Hey? Another tray here, please. Wonderful. Thanks.

Old Merna, eh boys? She's a big woman now, God bless her. Merna the Meat Muncher they call her now. Nobody's fool. She wanted to get married something awful at one time, you know. But she wouldn't go out with me, would she? Yous know that story? But then I haven't seen some of you fellas here before, have I? Yous must be new. You wouldn't know John-Angus then, eh? My brother, well, my step-brother. Now *he* was a tough customer. Ever hear of him?

It's like the other night when I grabbed a hold of Merna. Popped me right here. My God that was comical. I was nearly pissing myself. I grabbed on to her as she was going by the pool table there and I give her this smile and didn't she just lay off and hit me! Couldn't believe it. Couldn't believe Merna'd do something like that. The old Meat Muncher, eh Merna? You got to like it. Jesus.

But it's sad is what it is. Fucking hell, what a way to end up. You remember Merna from a few years back? No, maybe you fellas wouldn't remember. You'd never know it to see her today but old Merna was something. Just beautiful. Seriously. Right slim and dark-haired. She looked just like a girl of sixteen for so long, always wearing pink colourful clothes and that. Jesus, she was the most beautiful thing you ever saw and it was funny in a way because she was so shy and quiet back then. Right shy and fey she was, too.

Weren't you, Merna? I know you're listening over there. Behind the bar. I seen you. I seen your ears perk up. You remember all this better than me, hey.

But yes we used to come here quite a bit. I remember coming here with John-Angus and him saying Merna looked like she just walked out of a song or something. Every night he'd say something like that. He was always paying little attentions to Merna. John-Angus, he was just like me, couldn't ever resist a pretty face. God, I can still picture the two of them staring at each other for so long, talking to each other. I guess John-Angus had a little something for Merna. I guess we all did. Old John-Angus. He sure had a way with the ladies. They would've done anything for him, gone anywhere with him. He had something on Merna all right.

But really it's a sad story, my God, it's a tragic story is what it is. I'll never forget it. Never forget it. That's where I got this limp at. See, old John-Angus, he was a big, fine-looking fella. Not that big, but he *looked* big, you know. He was a crazy, violent kind of man and there was a lot of things strange about him. You just never know what's going on in someone's head. He could be a bastard, that's for sure. He was just a hard man to get to know. I never always got along with him too good. We practically hated each other sometimes. He had a real mean streak in him. But Jesus, he had the girlfriends by the dozens till he went and had to marry Kelsey-Lynn. Kelsey-Lynn McKay, eh? Poor Kelsey-Lynn. And she miscarried them first two anyways. The way it goes.

But even Kelsey-Lynn told me later she never really knew him, her own husband. That John-Angus always kept to himself and that. It was too hard to talk to him, she'd say. Like you could never get to know him. Like he wasn't listening to you. You know that feeling?

It was all because it was his father, if you want to know. I know, John-Angus told me. That night after the canoe races he was telling me all about it. His father, that would be Big Ranald, John-Angus told me no matter how hard he tried he couldn't ever get along with his own father. He was too strict and religious and that. Well my God, John-Angus started down the mine when he was only fifteen years old.

Think of it. So he was different all right. He was wild where his father wasn't. And when Big Ranald died, that's when Ma remarried and had us.

The biggest mistake of her life? I heard that. I heard that, Merna. How would you go and say a thing like that for, eh? Just mind your own business over there, woman.

The mines are closed now, of course, but my Christs we worked hard back then. We were working number twenty-six in Glace Bay, me and John-Angus. Cutting coal with a shear. That rock drill was heavy as hell and sat on your arm all day for eight hours straight. John-Angus's arm was huge on account of it. Big as my leg. She wasn't packing shelves at K-Mart then, boys. And me and John-Angus, we were always competing. He hated being beat something unbelievable.

But I got to tell you. That night after the canoe races, well me and John-Angus must've had fifty draft between the two of us. And this is when all those Indians come down from Whycocomagh, eh? All drunked up off of Aqua Velva or God knows what. With knives and all. These were the big ones, you know? Well I go out there into the parking lot, and, my God, didn't they just lit into me? I could hardly stand up let alone fight and here they were just a pounding and pounding on me. Blow after blow. Pummelling. I got banged up something terrible.

So John-Angus comes out just enraged with anger, yelling names and I never seen anything like it. I was on the ground there and Lord Jesus I seen a lot of fights but I never seen anyone that mad. This look come into his face, he was whirling around, swearing in Gaelic, I seen him grab hold of a man like this, right here in the groin and throw him. With one hand! Just a crazy, crazy night. Well, I got up and he knocked me over and was punching on me, everybody. Didn't care. Merna or somebody had to come out and stop it, people said.

And could he drink? I guess he could drink. He could out-drink you fellas any day. He could drink more than anyone I ever saw. Well both Ma and Kelsey-Lynn said he'd do himself in with drink. But he never listened to her. Or anybody. Had his fun, I guess. But he could be a right bastard to Kelsey-Lynn, true enough. True enough. She might've got slapped around a bit, too, and that ain't right. Different time.

Anyways, yes, John-Angus drunk me under the table too many nights to count. He drank like the devil and it was the strangest thing. He told me once, and I believe it, he said he drank himself sober rather than drunk. It was the only way, he said. Because he saw things. Visions and that. Snakes and all kinds of blustering ugly faces coming after him. You can joke about it now but it was different then no matter how you look at it.

But I can't figure it out. I could never figure it out. Holy Suffering Jesus Christ. Just happened I phoned in sick that day. This was in February, week after Valentine's, we were working along the north wall and this one day John-Angus decides to go for three runs in one shift, right? But you see, you can't do that, everybody knew that, but you're down there that long, this was after midnight, your mind starts playing head games on you. And the methane, that's the thing with methane, you can't see it, can't smell it, you don't know how much is around you but the shear hits sandstone, just one little spark and – *shoomph* – that fire shot up the wall three hundred feet, roaring along the rock face, flames everywhere, coal dust on fire –

And John-Angus, he was all set up to go on a vacation, you know. That night he and some other guy were going on a trip somewheres. I know, he was talking about it with me, smiling about it. So then they got the phone working from the surface, John-Angus still alive down there God knows how, spitting up snot and blood, but by this time the fire spread to the top levels of the mine. Poor buddy's down there by himself. No way out. Kids come to the phone. Kelsey-Lynn just couldn't bring herself to talk to him, Ma said. So I guess he says goodbye to the kids as long as the connection holds. Jesus Christ on the cross, eh?

I was here at the Legion when I got the call from Ma. I was sitting over there by the pay phones, sitting on this pink suitcase. I won't forget that, eh? Ma telling me that John-Angus was trapped down the mine, my own brother. I remember Merna running up to me when she heard me talking, running up to me like in a dream or something, all dressed up in a brand-new hat. But she was looking right straight into my eyes, reading my thoughts, figuring everything out without me saying nothing.

That was a big thing. That was the last for John-Angus. Like all of us, I guess. Some day. You get older or you don't. My brother got caught down a mine. And they sucked the air out of number twenty-six but she's still burning now. Still burning! Imagine, all that coal burning itself six miles out under the ocean.

John-Angus, he probably starved to death. Or the fire spread. Maybe he got the shear working and he drilled till the sea come in. Could've drownded, I guess. He was taken from us, Ma said. Her John-Angus. Never going to see another one like him. Never forget him. Never forget him. Not the same without him, Lord, no.

Yous coming with that fucking tray of beer or what, Merna? What the fuck's going on, woman? What are you sniffling over there, are yous? And you can stop with the staring anytime now. Yeah, well, have it your way, Merna. You have it your way.

But a pair of huge tits over there, fellas. Just huge. And yous can't get this next round, can you? I think I'm all out.

The Best Fuck in Laurel Canyon

SHE HAS FOUR DAYS LEFT on the movie, scattered over the next twelve days, and then a three-week gap in her schedule her agent wants her to fill. But she's *exhausted.* It's Friday evening, after wrap, and, as she walks up to her rental house, she sees on the doorstep two script-sized couriered packages. This is, in case you're wondering, Samantha Robbins, movie star. "Bright-eyed and glowing" were the character descriptions in the screenplays she was once sent. Descriptions now, eleven years later, trend more towards "alluring district attorney" or "gorgeous forensic pathologist." If you happen to see her in person, like the driver who just dropped her off, you'd come away thinking Samantha Robbins was confident, preoccupied, and possessed by some unquantifiable charisma. It's a charisma on full display even as she stoops with vague restlessness to grab the two packages. Holding them under her arm, along with a scribbled-on call sheet, Monday's sides, and a bottle of Evian water, she unlocks the front door and strides in, tossing her chattels on a kitchen countertop.

She moves to the refrigerator, pulls it open, and scans its contents: three more bottles of Evian, a bottle of California Chardonnay, and an unopened pack of Marlboro Ultra Lights. Taking out the wine and cigarettes, Samantha sets them on a counter. She grabs a wineglass from a cupboard and pours herself a full glass of wine. She brings this wine into the living room, placing it on a glass-and-chrome coffee table. From the pockets of her red blazer, she removes two cell phones – a new iPhone and a vintage BlackBerry – drops them on the coffee table, then lies down on the sofa. She twitches in discomfort a few moments before finding within the sofa cushions a vibrating massage wand. She yanks it out and examines it in a sort of oh-that's-where-that-went way. She's still considering it when a nearby cordless phone begins to ring. She does not move to answer it, however, and simply reclines again on the sofa, this time with the vibrating massage wand held to her chest. No sooner does the cordless phone stop ringing than the iPhone jingles. It is only when the iPhone goes quiet, and the BlackBerry's ring tone begins, that Samantha, like a pharaoh with a scepter, rises from the sofa and picks up the BlackBerry.

"This better be urgent," she says. "I'm in the middle of a very important decision."

"Sam! You all right?" The voice was full of concern. "You didn't answer your phones."

"I thought it was somebody else."

"Who would have all your numbers?"

She puts the vibrating massage wand on the coffee table. "What's up, Bryan?"

"We need clarity on a few things –"

"Join the party."

"You got a month-long hole in your schedule. Want to fill it? We need to decide now."

"I thought it was three weeks."

"I got them to move up your last day. Your picture wrapped a week early. Now you got a month."

"You maybe want to *tell* me you're doing this shit first?"

"They're not big scenes, honey. Shoe leather."

"Hey, when I walk up to a crack house, that's four years of Juilliard walking up to a crack house."

"Did you read the scripts I sent you?"

"I've been home forty-two seconds. I haven't even had a cigarette."

"Please don't smoke, Sam. With these digital cameras they see every pore, every line."

"It's called video retouching, Bryan."

"But you're drinking water? Promise me you're drinking water."

"I'm drinking –" Samantha reaches for her wineglass. "I promise you. What are the scripts?"

"The first is Errol's studio picture. The one on red paper."

Bending forward, Samantha pulls off her pumps. "I hate these fucking red scripts. I know it's security and everything but why do we have to kill trees? I can read this shit on my phone. And the first draft sucked."

"All first drafts suck."

"I don't want to do those roles anymore. It's basically 'Look at My Tits in Monument Valley.' What about Matthew's project? I loved it."

"They didn't get back to me. I think we would've heard by now. If you want, I can email."

"Email," says Samantha. "Go for clarity."

"Doing it –" There is a sound of rapid typing. "Did it. Now what about the fundraiser for what's-her-nuts? What do I tell her?"

"She wants me to host for free?"

"They'll send a car."

"Fuck, Bryan, I don't want to nickel-and-dime these idiots. If they paid me something, I'd do it. If it was a close friend, I'd do it. But I don't have any close friends. So fuck it." She drinks from the wine. "What about the indie movie?"

"I sent that over, too. It's scale. Three weeks. They need to know by Monday."

"It's scale? Can I bring Jean-Luc?"

"It's all freebies and favours, Sam. They have no money. If you want your own hair and makeup, you'd have to pay for it."

"For three weeks? I'd *lose* money." She makes a vague frown. "Who's the DP? Have you seen a reel?"

"I sent you the link."

"Just tell me what's up."

"I honestly didn't watch all of it. It's very spooky. Upside-down bustiers and black eyeliner and, you know, tortured souls in love with the darkness."

"And I'd be an alcoholic junkie vampire?"

"You'd be an alcoholic junkie vampire who dies on page sixty-three."

"Do I want to go to New Orleans, though?" Samantha sighs. "I think I need something else. I've just done three movies back to back, dude. I don't even know what city I'm waking up in anymore."

"You're in LA and you're a genius."

"There's just so much stupidity in my life right now. And I don't see any indication it's going away. In fact, I think it's getting worse."

"Almost forgot. I have another package here from your mother –"

"My mother?" Samantha flinches. "What is it this time?"

"Looks like vitamins. You want me to send it over? You told me not to forward anything."

"If I have to come in to sign something, I'll get it then."

"Shit."

"What?"

"Matthew's people just emailed back. They went another way with the part."

"Those fucks," says Samantha. "Fuck, I hate this industry. Why'd I go to his kid's birthday party?"

"Because you're a brilliant human being who inspires millions of people every day."

"I don't need this crap in my life, Bryan."

"When's your call on Monday?"

"I think pickup's at seven. Let me check." Standing up, and holding her BlackBerry to her cheek, Samantha moves to the kitchen to look at her call sheet. "Yup. Seven."

"I'll call you at wrap. Read those scripts. You're a genius!"

"Yeah?" Samantha notices a scribbled note and phone number at the top of her call sheet. "I think I know what I actually need."

"What's that?"

"Bye, Bryan! Talk soon."

TWENTY MINUTES LATER and Samantha is on a third cigarette, a second glass of wine, and halfway through a first reading of *Thunder Creek*, the script printed on dark red pages. More than a few times she has glanced at the scribbled note at the top of her call sheet and she is, in fact, reading it again, and reaching for her iPhone, when the iPhone starts to ring. Recognizing the number on the call display, she answers with a smirk. "Dear God," she says, "*finally*."

"Hello?" The voice is male: distinct, comforting, with a suggestion of mischief. "And how is Samantha Robbins tonight?"

"Waiting for you, freak," says Samantha. "Where are you?"

"Not sure. Limbo somewhere."

"Did your flight get out of London?"

"Just second. I think I see a sign. I'm somewhere called Lookout Mountain Avenue."

With the iPhone to her cheek, Samantha walks barefoot to the front door and opens it. There, nine steps below on the walkway, with an iPhone to *his* ear, is the actor, director, and producer Paul Bloom. He wears a dark suit and white dress shirt. Under his arm, he carries a sturdy brown paper bag from the Canyon Country Store. It's packed with tulips, takeout salads, and bottles of red and white wine. He smiles – a smile familiar to moviegoers the world over – and is about to speak when Samantha scream-whispers, "Jesus, man. Get *in* here before someone recognizes you."

Inside, he puts the bag of groceries in the kitchen and surveys the room, taking note of the red script, the glass of white wine, and the vibrating massage wand on the coffee table. "Sam," he says, "if you're in the middle of something, I can come back."

She closes the front door, turns to look at him, and shakes her head at the absurdity of the situation. "Come give me a kiss, you freak."

She moves to him on tippytoe and fondly kisses him on the lips.

Paul takes a step back, the better to look her in the eye, and nods at her wineglass. "You started without me?"

"I never know if you're going to show up."

"Didn't I tell you I was coming?"

"You drunk texted me from Heathrow." She moves to a cupboard and picks out a wineglass. "White or red?"

"Red's fine."

Samantha peeks into the bag of groceries. "Thanks for bringing wine, you charming bastard."

"I love that general store." Paul watches Samantha open the red wine with a corkscrew. "It's always the last place to get wine before the canyon."

She fills the wineglass. "Are you exhausted?"

"Not too bad. A little jet-lagged."

"But not so jet-lagged you're going to fall asleep, right?"

"Why? What're you doing later?"

"It's not what I'm doing later. It's *who* I'm doing later." She passes him the red wine. "And I'm choosing you."

"Hmm. Bold choice."

"So you can have one drink. And then you're fucking me."

"Ah," says Paul, "you can take the girl out of Pittsburgh –"

"Sewickley, yo. Sewickley." Samantha grabs her wineglass and raises it. "Cheers, Paul Bloom." She bumps her glass into his and gazes into his eyes. "My *God*, I like seeing you."

"And how about you?" He drinks from the red wine. "How was your day?"

"Oh, I like Fridays. I'm a Good Samaritan on Fridays."

"Who'd you save?"

"Because I'm not a resident anymore, they rent me this place –"

"Nice place."

"And I get a per diem so at the end of the week I raffle away all my per diems so the crew has something to look forward to on Friday."

"A free six hundred bucks? *I'm* looking forward to it. How do I get in on this?"

"Get an erection, I'll consider it. Get an erection, you're in."

He puckers his lips. "Hard bargain."

"If only. Is it too much to bend a girl over for a little hard bargain?"

"So what about the raffle? Who won today?"

"The key grip," says Samantha. "Trevor. He's two hundred and five pounds. Lean."

"Sounds like a choice cut."

"*And* he's an Ultimate Fighter." Samantha finds the call sheet and brings it to Paul. "He gave me his phone number and look what he wrote me."

Paul takes the call sheet and reads aloud the scribbled note: "'Want to help me spend it?' Smooth."

"Got to admire a man who goes for it."

"Wait – Trevor?" Paul flips over the call sheet and reads through a list of crew members by department. "Trevor Haas? *I* know Trevor Haas. When I did my first series, Trevor Haas was the grip. At lunch, we'd all smoke dope in the grip truck. He fucking hit on everybody. He fucking hit on *me*. Not to burst your bubble, Sam."

"Hmm-mmm," says Samantha, finishing her white wine. "Two hundred and five pounds."

"Now," says Paul, "are you hungry? I brought three kinds of salad –"

Grabbing the Marlboro Ultra Lights, Samantha twists her mouth, mock-annoyed. "This is the worst affair in the history of this city. What happened to all the sneaking around and crazy sex?" She fingers out a cigarette. "And motels in the afternoon and crazy sex?" She places the cigarette in her mouth and feels her jeans for her lighter. "And rose petals on the bed and crazy sex?"

"Didn't I bring tulips?"

"Just for once" – leaving the unlit cigarette in her mouth, Samantha slaps her hands on either side of her jeans zipper – "put your two lips here and suck me. Then fuck me. For God's sake, Paul. Do I have to beg?"

"Hmm," says Paul cautiously, "I'm waiting for the other shoe to drop."

"What about my pants? Are you waiting for my pants to drop? Here –" Samantha undoes her jeans and lets them fall to the floor. "Paul, I'm one of the hottest bitches in the city, I'm on Maxim's Hot 100 list, and you're talking about three kinds of salad?"

"Bullshit you're on Maxim's list."

"Google me, Paul. With or without lubricant. I don't care."

"Cool." He sips from his red wine and, with his other hand, pulls out his iPhone. "I got this. I'm on it."

"I just – seriously –" Locating her lighter on the kitchen countertop, Samantha lights her cigarette. "What kind of affair *is* this? I'm the best fuck in Laurel Canyon. You're supposed to fuck me. How do you not know this? Go read 'Adultery For Dummies' and then come back."

Paul glances up from his iPhone. "Is there an audio-book?"

"God, I hate you sometimes." Holding the lighter aloft, Samantha carelessly pitches it at his head.

Paul lifts his wineglass to shield his face and – though the lighter misses him completely – the abruptness of this movement slops red wine on the button placket of his white shirt. "Whoa, lady," he says, walking to the kitchen and removing his suit jacket. "This is a four-hundred-dollar shirt." At the sink, he lays his suit jacket on the counter. He unbuttons his shirt and takes it off, revealing a very well-defined physique.

"Holy *fuck*," says Samantha, staring at him. "Hold up. Don't move." She sets her cigarette on the rim of a very full ashtray, steps out of her fallen jeans, and walks towards him. "Would you look at you?" She scratches a fingernail down the centre of his chest. "That is fucking ridiculous."

"You like the superhero look, do you? Two-a-day workouts. You should see my carbs."

"I'd *love* to see your carbs. Show me your carbs. I'll get down on my knees if you show me your carbs."

Paul runs cold water over the spot of red wine, squirts some dish soap on it, then rinses the stain clean. He is pulling his shirt back on when Samantha, returning to take a drag of her cigarette, raises her hand.

"Sweetie," she says in a babyish voice, "please don't put your clothes back on. Please, please, *please?*"

"I don't know," says Paul, reaching for his suit jacket, "I just feel sort of naked without my clothes on."

"Fine. Done." Samantha squashes out her cigarette, sits

on the sofa, and picks up her iPhone. "Moving on." She leans forward and grabs the call sheet. "Oh, Trevor. You Ultimate Fighter, you."

"We sexting Trevor? I can help with that."

"You're going to help me sext Trevor, are you?"

"Sure. I'm all about sexting. And emojis."

"Here –" She slides her iPhone along the coffee table. "Send it from mine. We'll write it together."

"Sweet." Paul picks up the iPhone. "How flirty off the top? Something simple? 'Sup bae?' That work for you?"

"I actually believe you would do this."

"Oh, I'm willing to go pretty far. But I draw the line at dick pics. Let's just say –" He whistles. "Lesson learned."

"Are you serious?" Samantha sits up, her eyes bright with interest. "Did you?" She stares at him. "You can tell me. I won't tell. Who'd you send it to?"

"It was just a misunderstanding between myself and another person."

"You still have it?"

"The pic or the dick? I think I have *one* of them?" Paul touches at the pockets of his suit jacket. "Somewhere."

Giggling now, Samantha continues to stare at him. "Fuck, you're cute. But my *God* you drive me crazy. I want to smack you and kiss you and fuck you all at the same –" She shivers. "Ech. Too many feelings."

"You want to talk about it?"

"My feelings? Yeah. That's why I invited you here. Why don't you talk to my mother? You'd be better off."

"What's her number?"

"Oh, Ida would be thrilled. She doesn't know I know you. Give her something to talk about at bingo."

Paul scrolls through the contacts on her iPhone. "Wait. Here it is –"

"Except for the fact that she loves your wife. She tried to send me your wife's fucking cookbook. Jesus, did that piss me off."

"I'm guessing it's 'Mom'?"

"Wait –" Realizing he's already started a call, Samantha abruptly gets up. "No, you don't. You do not. Paul!"

She grabs at her iPhone but he sidesteps her so the coffee table is between them.

"Hello," Paul says into the iPhone, "is that Ida? It's Paul Bloom –"

From the iPhone's earpiece, Samantha hears the burble of her mother's voice. And with her mother's voice are conjured images of her mother's unchanging kitchen – the yellow push-button telephone with the long curling cord, the empty beer bottles on the checkered linoleum floor, the Formica table with the crooked dent in its chrome frame, a dent that matches the scar on Samantha's forehead, a memento from the time she first ran away.

"I'm in a restaurant with Samantha and her pals," Paul is saying, "and she was talking about calling you. And Ida? I'm just going to put you on speaker –"

Paul puts the iPhone in the centre of the coffee table. From its speaker, Samantha now hears her mother switching to her politest voice: "Isn't she in the middle of a filming?"

"No, no. She's here in the restaurant. Somewhere. There she is."

"Sammy?"

"Hi, Mom."

"Samantha, you never told me you knew Paul Bloom!"

"Didn't I?"

"Now, Ida –" Paul takes the call sheet and rattles it above the iPhone. "I'm looking at the dessert menu, so what do you think we should get? Gâteau au chocolat. Can't go wrong with chocolate cake. Maybe crème brûlée?"

"You're in the middle of dinner?"

"I don't know if you like crème brûlée."

"What is it?"

"It's like custard with caramel. Would you like one?" Looking over his shoulder and, as if talking to an assistant, Paul says, "Bradley, can we send one of these to Sam's mother?"

"Oh, you don't have to do that!"

"You sure?"

"It's too far to send a dessert. From California?"

"Cancel that, Bradley." Paul turns to Samantha. "And Sam, you're okay with just the latte?"

"Hmm-mmm."

"Oh, she *never* gets dessert."

"So, Ida, tell me," says Paul warmly, "how was the day in Sewickley?"

"Well, we had a little rain this afternoon –"

"You have a chance to get out for a walk?"

"I've had a bit of a scratchy throat I've been trying to get rid of. I'm supposed to see the doctor – I have an appointment next week – but *I* never know."

"Have you tried tea with honey?"

"Lord, no. Turns my stomach. You're not a tea-and-honey person, are you, Paul?"

"More of a red wine man."

"I suppose I could try that."

"Let me know how he turns out."

There is a quick hoot of laughter from Samantha's mother, a delighted tone Samantha has not heard in some time – years, really – and, as she reaches for her pack of cigarettes, for some reason she presses her lips together very, very tightly.

"Now, Ida," says Paul, "I don't know if Sam tells you about all the generous things she does for people."

"Well, no, she doesn't. She doesn't tell me, Paul."

"She keeps things pretty quiet. But she does a lot of good in the world. She brightens a lot of people's day." Paul flicks at the faded stain on his button placket. "I know Sam's in the middle of this dinner meeting so we should let her get back to that."

"Well, Paul, I just thank you for taking time out of your day to call me."

"You kidding?" Paul turns with a smile to Samantha. "What else would I be doing?" He bends over the iPhone. "You have a great night, Ida."

"Well, I will *now*. You just made an old woman very happy. Is Samantha still there? Are you still there, Sammy?"

"Yup," says Samantha, "if you can believe it."

"Did you do that? Did you get Paul to call me?"

"Oh, Mom. You know as well as I do. You can never get a man to do anything. They have to think it's their idea. *Then* they might get around to doing something. No, they have minds of their own. At least, they think they do."

"Well, you're being very sweet and thank you, Sammy." Her mother's voice begins to quaver with emotion. "It's a lovely surprise. You know, your father and I are *so* proud of you and everything you've accomplished. We love you very much. And did you get the vitamin D drops I sent you?"

"Yup."

"And you're taking them? Two drops underneath your tongue?"

"Two drops. Underneath my tongue. Love you, too. Say hi to Dad."

"I will. Take care now."

Paul leans over the iPhone. "Bye, Ida!"

Samantha touches a button to end the call. She is silent a moment. Then, without taking out a cigarette, she puts the pack of cigarettes on the coffee table.

"Now," says Paul, "that wasn't so bad, was it?"

"If you do this," says Samantha, her eyes moist with tears, "if you make me fall in love with you, I swear to God, Paul Bloom, I'll never forgive you."

"The other shoe."

"You understand me? I won't."

"I see." He comes over and sits down beside her. "Any plans for the weekend?" Looking into her eyes, he takes her hand in his. "What're you doing later?"

Ordinary
Love Song

From: Byron Wu <mailto: byronwu1982@hotmail.com>
Sent: Wednesday, April 2, 2003 11:59 PM
To: Postings at Guitar Tablatures <postings@gtabs.com>
Subject: New song

Does anybody have guitar tabs for the new Blue Wonder song? Just heard it on CBC's RadioSonic. I don't know what it's called and never heard it before. Sounds like it's mostly G and C chords and ringing open strings before the fuzz box part. Anyone?

From: Jessica Ryder <jessee@interdirect.ca>
Sent: Tuesday, April 8, 2003 10:20 PM
To: Byron Wu <byronwu1982@hotmail.com>
Subject: Re: New song

That song is amaaazing! it's called ordinary lovesong and it's prolly the first release off their new cd that i don't know the title of—but love the fuzzy dreampop—the song's for sure in g major and that opening progression is 1-5-6-6 with repeating open g and b strings. the little bridge sounds like c-bm-d which leads to the pretty verse part which sounds easy but i'd have to hear it again to know for sure—or see them when they come to canada!
ciao,
jessica

From: Byron Wu <byronwu1982@hotmail.com>
Sent: Wednesday, April 9, 2003 11:22 PM
To: Jessica Ryder <jessee@interdirect.ca>
Subject: Re: re: New song

Hi Jessica
Thanks for replying to that post! I heard the song on the radio again and you're completely right about the opening chord progression. It's G-D-Em-Em. And the pretty verse part is sliding C-shape open chords up and down the neck. And maybe there's an open Em in there as well? Sounds like it.
Best,
Byron Wu
P.S. How do you know they're touring? I have a friend who writes for Exclaim magazine in Toronto but he didn't know. (I'm in Canada, too. What are the odds?)

From: Jessica Ryder <jessee@interdirect.ca>
Sent: Wednesday, April 23, 2003 2:19 AM
To: Byron Wu <byronwu1982@hotmail.com>
Subject: Re: re: re: New song

hey there b
Finally checked my emails of last two weeks—my life SO in flux right now—Blue Wonder are playing the Horseshoe in June as part of NXNE festival—who's your friend at Exclaim?
jess
ps The Odds are a Vancouver band ;)

From: Byron Wu <byronwu1982@hotmail.com>
Sent: Thursday, April 24, 2003 6:11 PM
To: Jessica Ryder <jessee@interdirect.ca>
Subject: Re: re: re: re: New song

Hi Jessica
My friend at Exclaim is Ash Jindal. He's the art director. I just got an email from him explaining that, yes, Blue Wonder play North by Northeast on June 6. When I told him your question, he said: "Ask her if it's Jess from Trent who goes out with Caleb."
Byron

From: Jessica Ryder <jessee@interdirect.ca>
Sent: Friday, April 25, 2003 5:30 PM
To: Byron Wu <byronwu1982@hotmail.com>
Subject: !!!

U MEAN ASH WHO LIVES WITH GEMMA!!!??? THAT IS SO WEIRD!!!! what *ARE* the odds of all the emails flying around a guitar tabs website it's people connected by friends? that seriously, seriously messes with my brain and makes me think you guys are all watching me type this! I just called Gemma and—doo-doo doo-doo—she said she knew you when you guys were at Guelph together? that is, if you're the brilliant Byron from the Photo Arts Club who once pulled three all-nighters in a row! : o

She said you should come to her birthday drinks so you'll prolly get an invite from her. ok i share ur email with her? I dunno—is this weird? its like guitar tabs slash internet personals? And prolly somebody is really a spambot and not telling the other ;o)
Jess
(who did go to Trent but doesn't go out with Caleb anymore)

From: Byron Wu <byronwu1982@hotmail.com>
Sent: Monday, April 28, 2003 10:21 PM
To: Jessica Ryder <jessee@interdirect.ca>
Subject: Re: !!!

Birthday gatherings? Not sure. My life is pretty hectic. Between studying for the GMAT and trying to figure out the picking pattern in Radiohead's "Let Down," I barely have enough time to make Ichiban. Plus I may have a head cold. If I don't make it, say hey to Gemma for me.
Cheers,
Byron

From: Jessica Ryder <jessee@interdirect.ca>
Sent: Tuesday, April 29, 2003 8:03 PM
To: Byron Wu <byronwu1982@hotmail.com>
Subject: Hey.

Hey B
cool to see you at gemma's and sorry i had to dash—it was just a strange day for me personally—just normal human stuff—i've been basically trying to quit all intoxicants not to mention i have to take a break from all things Peterborough—i mean I love the patch but I just felt a rant coming on and couldn't deal—trying to move on, you know? Apparently you learn more from your mistakes—in which case, I should be a genius by now ;)
peace in the middle east,
J

From: Byron Wu <byronwu1982@hotmail.com>
Sent: Tuesday, April 29, 2003 10:21 PM
To: Jessica Ryder <jessee@interdirect.ca>
Subject: Re: Hey.

> but I just felt a rant coming on
Which rant? I'm still waiting on Ichiban, I gave up on Radiohead, and I've done enough sample Integrated Reasoning questions for one week. So I have the time. Which rant?

From: Jessica Ryder <jessee@interdirect.ca>
To: Byron Wu <byronwu1982@hotmail.com>
Sent: Tuesday April 29, 2003 11:28 PM
Subject: Re: re: Hey

well, not to be a complete girl but I was sort of having a major wtf moment—the vibe can be so HEAVY at those Trent parties & i always feel this brutal, soul-crushing ennui when I'm surrounded by all the indie feel-the-painers. Basically there's sort of this archetype for people from Trent—the indie-rock dude at the back of the party in the plaid shirt drinking PBR who sees the truth in all the blood and spit and despair as he bumblefucks his way through a philosophy degree but drops out fourth year and moves to Kensington Market and plays in five different bands and always decries the new big thing as the next big shit because how can anything popular possibly be good? meanwhile he goes to every hipster bingo night like he's a totally sane together guy only doing an impersonation of a doofy crazy person when in ACTUAL FACT he's just a fragile little boy lost without his muff pedal—look i do like sensitive boy rock—the first treble charger was genius—but i also love EDM and Darkwave and Hip-Hop and i wouldn't categorize my Trent friends majorly in this category but it's trippy-ass shit with a social message—and I also know arguing about pop music is prolly the biggest waste of time in the world—it's really about whatever moment you're in—but sometimes the difference between where people are and where they want to be *is* sort of a soul-crushing ennui for me—okay THERE rant officially over —your ichiban noodles are probably burned by now : /
oops,
jess
p.s. there may be a Matador plan for Fri nite if Quinn and I have any energy after our bar shifts—u around?

From: Byron Wu <byronwu1982@hotmail.com>
Sent: Thursday, May 1, 2003 11:29 AM
To: Jessica Ryder <jessee@interdirect.ca>
Subject: Matador

What is this Matador? Do I need a cape or sword? Do you mean the after-hours place where the Leonard Cohen video was filmed? It's at Dovercourt and College? Please advise.

From: Jessica Ryder <jessee@interdirect.ca>
Sent: Tuesday, May 6, 2003 3:59 PM
To: Byron Wu <byronwu1982@hotmail.com>
Subject: Re: Matador

byron you are fucking LEGEND when you get going!!! was it a full moon? And how weird was that when we walked past Pizza Pizza at 4 AM some pimped-out Honda Civic drives by with the new Blue Wonder track bumping? is this fate or what i need to know :)

The art opening thingee on Thursday you were talking about at the end of the night—can I get back to you on that by the end of the week?—it's just you may not hear from me as i am BUSY—finally sucked it up and quit bartending—that's right—ur looking at Jess the Temp till I find something more perminent—and also biting another bullet and looking for an apartment—don't think i can stay with Quinn any longer—she and her fiance are so uber-coupley and connubial it's like "Quinn, come out for one drink?" "Honestly I can't—we have to get up early to get the best parking place at Home Depot" i dunno, me, if I ever got married i just want a house with a theremin and an underground criminal lab—but if you can, please tell me a) why is the world full of cruel morons? b) why am I exhausted? c) will I ever find a place?
talk soon,
Jess

From: Jessica Ryder <jessee@interdirect.ca>
Sent: Thursday, May 8, 2003 3:59 PM
To: Byron Wu <byronwu1982@hotmail.com>
Subject: Re: re: re: re: New Song

hi Byron holy snappers am I tired—just looked at five grisly little apartments—one was semi-okay I mean granted it wasn't 100% ideal, but it was a house, on a quietish street, and not a run-down tenement suspended over a crime scene (which was what the place at College and Spadina was srsly like)... and to get back to you—i'm not really feeling that art opening and Quinn's bagged but do you wanna maybe have a drink *later* later? call me if u do. Here's my cell: 704-JESS

From: Jessica Ryder <jessee@interdirect.ca>
Sent: Friday, May 9, 2003 3:19 PM
To: Byron Wu <byronwu1982@hotmail.com>
Subject: Your Pad

byron—thanks for letting me sleep in yo—your place is so CLEAN and QUIET when you went to your appointment i fell back asleep for 2 more hours!!! & when i woke up i didn't know where i was (is it november, miami, summer—idk!) & yr apartment is totally a gateway into Byron Wu World—now I know you have:

a. A Gibson Les Paul in mint condition
b. A super-modular cool as fuck digital Nikon camera
c. one *less* pair of folded underwear in your top drawer—
   that's right I take a trophy prize from all my prey DUN DUN DUNNN

um, one further question, how do i connect you with that John the Babtist guy u used to be in your high school yearbook photo? And—wtf—did you graduate high school at 15? Is that even POSSIBLE? btw Quinn's away this wk so i think I'm just going to chill and watch the Buffy finale on video—maybe wanna come over later? call me?
x Jess

From: Byron Wu <byronwu1982@hotmail.com>
Sent: Friday, May 9, 2003 2:33 PM
To: Jessica Ryder <jessee@interdirect.ca>
Subject: Re: Your Pad

Should I bring wine? Wait. I'll call you. I'm calling you. Your cell's ringing. You just said "Hello." I'll stop typing now.

From: Jessica Ryder <jessee@interdirect.ca>
Sent: Saturday, May 10, 2003 3:19 PM
To: Byron Wu <byronwu1982@hotmail.com>
Subject: Re: re: Your Pad

Hey there—i just realized we never got around to ahem—actually watching the Buffy finale—we should really try to watch that some time—but hey! at least u didn't faint at the sight of blood! :p :p :p and sorry abt the hickeys but when I do ex I kind of lose my brain—actually I saw a Flintstones episode like that once when Fred ate pickled dodo bird egg and lost his brain—or maybe it was bubbles in the powerpuff girls—yeah, I think he ate bubbles. i await your call..........
xxxxxxxxxxxxxxxxxxxxxxxxxx
jess
if any of the photos u took aren't too pukey send me one pleeeeez?

From: Jessica Ryder <jessee@interdirect.ca>
Sent: Monday, May 12, 2003 3:19 PM
To: Byron Wu <byronwu1982@hotmail.com>
Subject: Monday Morning

Hey Byron!
Jessica Ryder here, the clock-watching temp, coming to you live through the Interdirect Website email program. I have been power-surfing the net on this office's direct link. It's a tad faster than my crappy laptop dial-up thingee. But hey don't think I'm not working!

Because already? I have filed nine fax cover sheets, delivered eight phone messages, inputted three pages of client feedback tracking and—wait for it—crashed the Microsoft Excel program! Only six more hours to go! So hey why don't you:

a. tell me three things you've never told anyone else
b. share with me a KitKat bar
c. call me on my cell and leave a dirty voice mail
d. call me at extension 221 and leave a dirty voice mail
e. press pound for more options ;-)

Peace and love and all of the above,
Jess
p.s. Have you ever been to High Park?

From: Byron Wu <byronwu1982@hotmail.com>
Sent: Wednesday, May 14, 2003 6:59 PM
To: Jessica Ryder <jessee@interdirect.ca>
Subject: Re: Monday Morning

Hey Jess
I love High Park but I'm slammed this week as I have my parents in town from Font Hill and their idea of fun is telling me what to do. And when. And how. To offer you a further glimpse into Byron Wu World: when I was twelve, I was given GMAT flashcards. As a birthday present. When I was *twelve*. Yeah. Anyway, let me rain check High Park this week but, as you may have noticed, I have begun to fulfill some of the items on your list!
See you soon if I survive.
Byron

From: Jessica Ryder <jessee@interdirect.ca>
Sent: Thursday, May 15, 2003 3:19 PM
To: Byron Wu <byronwu1982@hotmail.com>
Subject: a rainy night in may

byron wu
it is i
jessica ryder
wondering why
ur the guy
out in the city
when shouldn't you
be the man
in my bed?
it would be lovely
to see you again
if you have time
between excursions
xo
j

From: Byron Wu <byronwu1982@hotmail.com>
Sent: Friday, May 16, 2003 4:59 PM
To: Jessica Ryder <jessee@interdirect.ca>
Subject: Re: a rainy night in may

I am alive! Parents leaving in an hour. I have a surprise for you so keep Saturday June 6 free. Also: I think I have just purchased the biggest KitKat bar on the planet. And is your phone off or uncharged or something? I can't wait to see you!
xo
Byron

From: Jessica Ryder <jessee@interdirect.ca>
Sent: Saturday, May 17, 2003 1:19 AM
To: Byron Wu <byronwu1982@hotmail.com>
Subject: Re: re: a rainy night in may

Wu!
me so drunkie! after work went out with da sistahood and saw a ton of people we havn't seen in ages now haviong a little rompromtu drop-in at quinn's shrooms and tunes - she downloaded the blue wonder MP3 and burnt a CD for me so we have it on non-stop and infinite repeat it is the awesomeness BECAUSE THIS SONG & THIS SONG & NOTHING WILL EVR BE AS GOOD AS THIS SONG! & when the girl's voice comes in after that janglepop solo? just chills and a mix of sadness and joy and nostlgia and something else words cannot describe and I have no idea why or when & quinn's like "How does this song know so much about me?" :D :D :D hey how cum u never told me anything you never told anybody else? uh-oh gotta go - party zombies coming up the stairs! whre is u? I miss u Wu but I know you have to study for the exam c u soon honey hope you got loads o studying done tonite and alzo kitkat chocolatey goodness?
xo jss

From: Byron Wu <byronwu1982@hotmail.com>
Sent: Thursday, May 15, 2003 11:44 PM
To: Jessica Ryder <jessee@interdirect.ca>
Subject: You
Attach: Jess_Morning.tiff

> tell me three things you've never told anyone else

Jessica Ryder, I will tell you three things I've never told anyone else. First let me mention something I heard you say. When you were talking at the Matador with Quinn about relationships and breaking up and making up and you told her it doesn't really matter who's responsible or why it happens. What matters is that it happens at all. And I realize it is about whatever moment you're in because what else is there? Most of my life I've been preparing for the future, since I was six my parents have been preparing me for the future, but maybe seriously what I've been missing is the present.

So here's the first thing I've never told anyone else. And I don't mean to freak you out but I want to be honest about everything. I struggle with health issues and the possibility I may be clinically depressed or even slightly schizophrenic. Twice I've been hospitalized with a severe anxiety disorder. Just a ton of overthinking and focusing on things that imply failure and letting negative thoughts get in the way of everyone and everything. Does this have anything to do with a childhood where I was always three years younger than everyone else in my class? Probably. Or that, for my immigrant parents, emotions don't really exist? Probably. I don't know if I can explain it to someone who didn't live it but my parents don't really believe in emotions. They certainly don't believe in depression. They see it as frivolous sadness. But for an entire year, I went to bed with stomach pains and the feeling that no matter how hard I work or prepare things will never really work out and that my parents' ridiculously high expectations for me WILL CHANGE AS SOON AS I MEET THEM. And the idea that my own understanding of my life might be different than theirs seems like the most selfish thing and worst betrayal I could ever possibly do which is probably why I have had the same nightmare of falling through darkness, just endlessly falling through darkness, since I was twelve. (I've never told anyone that before either.)

But, Jess, you're full of light. That's why I have to keep looking at you. Just to confirm you're there. We've known each other two months, I can't believe we've been in the same city for three years before that, but in these two months I feel like I'm finally waking up from wherever the fuck i used to be.

On Saturday, when we woke up at your place, the blonde hair on your arm looked so beautiful on the blue futon in a shine of sunlight and while you slept on top of me I didn't know whose heartbeat I was hearing, yours or mine, and all of it was amazing because I was with you.

The photograph attached is from that moment. Just as you woke up. Here's the third thing I've never told anyone. I love you.
<3
Byron

From: Jessica Ryder <jessee@interdirect.ca>
Sent: Friday, May 16, 2003 7:46 PM
To: Byron Wu <byronwu1982@hotmail.com>
Subject: GAH!

hey Byron
ok—whatever you sent me CRASHED MY COMPUTER—just frozen scariness—so I had to delete Outlook Express and so now i have lost all my emails and—worse—all my email addresses WHICH REALLY SUCKS—but wait there's more—even after I reloaded the program there's some internal error and now I can't even get connected to the web???

So I drop off my crappy laptop to the Laboratory of Peculiar Repair Men and now I'm at Kinko's doing emails but apparently all the emails I sent today are getting lost in some alternate universe? so if you get this email twelve million times please don't loathe my existence, ok?

also listen—i should tell u—Caleb came to Quinn's on friday nite and I told him about us for the first time because one thing Caleb and I have never done to each other is lie & he wants to do the have-coffee-and-talk thing which means MORE Caleb head-games which obviously i do not want to do but I do have to get my stuff out of his place so I should prolly buckle up and do it— erkay—time to pick up my computer—wut did u send me anyway? was it a monster jpeg or something cuz when I clicked on the file the whole thing cacked out—idk maybe my laptop was doomed but I think I just couldn't handle the attachment.
c u
jess

From: Byron Wu <byronwu1982@hotmail.com>
Sent: Tuesday, May 20, 2003 8:01 PM
To: Jessica Ryder <jessee@interdirect.ca>
Subject: Re: GAH!

Computer trouble is the worst. If you need a laptop, I have a spare Toshiba satellite with a Pentium chip. It's only two years old. And in terms of the Caleb have-coffee-and-talk thing, if you have to see an ex, I can understand that.

> wut did u send me anyway?

It was a digital photograph of you. From the morning I first stayed over. Remember you asked me to send you a photo? I can get a hardcopy outputted. Were you able to read what I wrote? And, hey, just to be clear: June 6 is when Blue Wonder are playing The Horseshoe. We have tickets. So let me know that you got this email. And is your message box full on your cell?
miss you,
Byron

From: Jessica Ryder <jessee@interdirect.ca>
Sent: Sunday, May 25, 2003 3:33 PM
To: Byron Wu <byronwu1982@hotmail.com>
Subject: Re: re: GAH!

Hey Byron—sorry about the weirdness this evening—it's been another trip to catastrophe but Caleb officially goes on tour in a week so all that drama will be gone from the city he's never normally so belligerint & i'd appreciate if you do NOT repeat to anyone what he said if you heard it & sorry i'm so generally spaced lately i just have a lot of personal stuff going on not to mention I'm PISSED quinn's subletting this place for the rest of the summer which means i have to be gone by June 1st? AH! So i have to find a new place & a second job? AHH! & buy a new computer? AHHH! But of course that WOULD be ridiculously cool to see Blue Wonder at NXNE lemme sort myself out—i'll call you—when u around?
xxj

From: Mail Delivery System
Sent: Friday, June 5, 2003 11:21 PM
To: byronwu1982@hotmail.com
Subject: MAIL DELIVERY FAILED: RETURNING MESSAGE TO SENDER

This message was created automatically by mail delivery software. A message you sent could not be delivered to one or more of its recipients. The following address(es) failed: <jessee@interdirect.ca>:

This is a permanent error.
209.226.175.175 does not like recipient.
Remote host said: 501 #5.1.1 bad address jessee@interdirect.ca
Giving up on 209.226.175.175.
Return-Path: <byronwu1982@hotmail.com>
Received: (qmail 11064 invoked from network); 12 June 2003 16:33:18 -0000
b=I4EHcOHMGYAzqL3rFHbLhbJjmboAgGi/
SNBmIYWWE2mIEzzcYCnvTTZOHH7KUFOrlyXJK6z
DeNyzCbtRRZMBrP3S+AZMDL5zkEInc= ;
Message-ID: <000101c68406$bcdedc30$50a32a18@byron7vq78h9>
MIME-Version: 1.0
X-MimeOLE: Produced By Microsoft MimeOLE V6.00.2900.2869
This is a multi-part message in MIME format.

--- Below this line is a copy of the message ---

From: "Byron Wu" <byronwu1982@hotmail.com>
Sent: 4 Jun 2003 22:09:23
To: <jessee@interdirect.ca>
Subject: WHAT'S UP? ARE YOU OKAY?

>JESS
>ARE YOU MAD AT ME? DID I SAY OR DO SOMETHING
>THAT INSULTED YOU OR OFFENDED YOU IN SOME WAY? IF I DID
>I'M SORRY. BUT I DON'T KNOW WHAT I DID TO BE
>TREATED LIKE THIS OR WHY YOU CAN'T EVEN *TALK* TO ME
>ANYMORE OR CALL OR EVEN SEND AN EMAIL? WTF IF YOU DON'T WANT
>TO SEE
>ME, OKAY, I CAN UNDERSTAND THAT, BUT I'M WORRIED ABOUT YOU. ARE
>YOU OKAY? NO ONE'S SEEN YOU. I LEFT A MESSAGE FOR QUINN
>MAYBE SHE KNOWS WHERE YOU ARE BUT I JUST WANT TO KNOW YOU'RE
>OKAY. ARE YOU? BLUE WONDER
>PLAY TOMORROW
>X
>
>
> BYRON

From: Katje Wittemann <wittykat@web.de>
Sent: Friday, December 31, 2004 3:32 AM
To: Postings at Guitar Tablatures <postings@gtabs.com>
Subject: gewöhnliche liebeslied

I understand it is the most played earworm of the last year but I am nonetheless interested to know the tablatures for "Ordinary Love Song" by Die Blaues Wunder. I've managed most of it from watching the MTV video but I can't get some of the teeny bits of the guitar solo when the woman is singing. Weiß jemand?
viele Grüße
Katje in Mitte

From: Byron Wu <byron.wu@rotman.utoronto.ca>
Sent: Sunday, January 25, 2004 11:59 PM
To: Postings at Guitar Tablatures <postings@gtabs.com>
Subject: Re: gewöhnliche liebeslied

ORDINARY LOVE SONG by Blue Wonder

PART ONE – Intro
This is the guitar intro before the drums come in.

```
e ||------------|------------|------------|------------|
B ||----------0-|----------0-|----------0-|------------|
G ||-----0------|-----0------|-----0------|-----0------|
D ||------------|------------|------------|----------0-|
A ||------------|------------|------------|------------|
E ||-3-3---3-3--|-2-2---2-2--|-0-0---0-0--|-0-0---0-0--|

e ||------------|----------0-|------------|------------|
B ||----------3-|------------|----------3-|----------1-|
G ||-----0------|-----0------|-----0------|-----0------|
D ||------------|------------|------------|----------0-|
A ||------------|------------|------------|------------|
E ||-3-3---3-3--|-2-2---2-2--|-0-0---0-0--|-0-0---0-0--|

e ||----------3-|----------3-|----------3-|----------3-|
B ||----------0-|----------0-|----------0-|----------0-|
G ||-----0------|-----0------|-----0------|-----0------|
D ||------------|------------|------------|------------|
A ||------------|------------|------------|------------|
E ||-3-3---3-3--|-2-2---2-2--|-0-0---0-0--|-0-0---0-0--|
```

PART TWO – Bridge

This is the fuzz pedal part which is down-strumming C-Maj to B-Min to D-Maj power chords twice sitting on the D chord at the end and letting the fuzz sustain while the other guitar goes clear-tone for the first verse part.

PART THREE – First Verse

```
e ||------------|-0----------|------------|-0----------|
B ||-0----------|------------|-0----------|------------|
G ||----0----0-|---0----0---|-----0----0-|---0----0---|
D ||---9----9--|--4----2----|---9-----9--|--5----4----|
A ||-10---10---|-5----3-----|-10----10---|-7----5-----|
E ||------------|------------|------------|------------|
```

```
e ||------------|-0----------|------------|-0----------|
B ||-0----------|------------|-0----------|------------|
G ||----0----0-|---0----0---|-----0----0-|---0----0---|
D ||---9----9--|--4----2----|---9-----9--|--5----4----|
A ||-10---10---|-5----3-----|-10----10---|-7----5-----|
E ||------------|------------|------------|------------|
```

When I think of all the time I spent   Writing songs that never went anywhere

```
e ||------------|-0----------|-0----------|-0----------|
B ||-0----------|------------|------------|------------|
G ||----0----0-|---0----0---|-----0----0-|---0----0---|
D ||---9----9--|--4----2----|---9-----9--|--5----4----|
A ||-10---10---|-5----3-----|-10----10---|-7----5-----|
E ||------------|------------|------------|------------|
```

When all I ever really meant to mean   was everything to you

```
e ||------------|------------|------------|------------|
B ||------------|------------|------------|------------|
G ||---0----0---|---0---0----|---0---0----|---0---0----|
D ||--2---2-----|--4---4-----|--5---5---5-|--5---5---5-|
A ||-3---3---3--|-5---5---5--|-7---7---7--|-7---7---7--|
E ||------------|------------|------------|------------|
```

Where were we When we knew?

```
e ||------------|------------|------------|------------|
B ||------------|------------|------------|------------|
G ||---0----0---|---0---0----|---0---0----|---0---0----|
D ||--2---2-----|--4---4-----|--5---5---5-|--5---5---5-|
A ||-3---3---3--|-5---5---5--|-7---7---7--|-7---7---7--|
E ||------------|------------|------------|------------|
```

Where was I... And where... were... you?

```
e ||------------|------------|------------|
B ||------------|------------|------------|
G ||---0----0---|------------|----0-------|
D ||--2----4----|---0----0---|---2--------|
A ||-3--3-5--5--|--2----0----|--2---------|
E ||------------|-3--3-2---2-|-0----------|
```

Hiding in some afternoon not knowing every song was you

```
e ||------------|------------|------------|------------|
B ||------------|------------|------------|------------|
G ||---0--0-----|---0--0-----|---0--0-----|---0--0-----|
D ||--2--2--2---|--2--2--2---|--4--4--4---|--4--4--4---|
A ||-3--3--3----|-3--3--3----|-5--4--5----|-5--4--5----|
E ||------------|------------|------------|------------|
```

But every song... Every song... was... [you]

Then back to Part One and that opening riff. The other lyrics are hard to work out so I'll leave them to you. It's probably not important the song is 100% right. It's more about the moments.

Byron Wu
byron.wu@rotman.utoronto.ca
Rotman School of Management
University of Toronto

------------------------ PLEASE NOTE ------------------------
This file is the author's own work and represents their
interpretation of the song. You may only use this file for
private study, scholarship, or research. Remember to view
this file in Courier or some other monospaced font. See
http://www.guitartablatures.com/faq for more information.

Twyla

"I THINK WE'RE LIVING IN the Golden Age of Fuck Off. I really do. What the fuck even matters anymore? Because let me ask you a question, and I'm curious about this, when you talk to your other patients, who all look fucking crazy by the way, I've seen them in the lobby futzing with their Kleenex and how you even *talk* to those freaks is beyond me – it's called personal hygiene, people – but how many of your patients are just fed up with the rest of the world? Because you know on your laptop the X that appears in the corner of pop-up screens? I just want one of those. But for other people. So I can click on the X and they disappear and go back into the darkness. Do you know what I mean, though? What is with people? Ah, I fucking hate this week."

These remarks are coming toward the end of a third appointment with Dr. C. A. Symons – the third of an agreed-upon trial of six sessions of psychotherapy – and Twyla, the young woman speaking, dressed today in a black sheer blouse, pencil skirt, and ankle boots, is just now staring at herself in the mirror on the wall opposite. Or not staring so much as frowning. Her expression is that of someone who can't quite determine why something looks, as she might say, a little off. She fluffs her bangs. She scrunches her nose. Then, impulsive, she shifts herself on the sofa so she can no longer see her reflection.

In the chair opposite Twyla, Dr. Symons looks at her inquisitively, as if awaiting further details.

"Oh," says Twyla, "it's nothing. It's just I never look good in that mirror and it drives me crazy but whatever."

Dr. Symons crosses her legs at the knee and positions her notebook on her lap. "You were talking about your week. What happened this week?"

"Oh, you know. My dad's in the hospital. My relationship's in limbo. I hate all my friends. The usual. I think I want to move somewhere where I won't be bothered by other people's lives." Twyla watches Dr. Symons jot down a note. "But I need to ask you something."

"What's that?"

"Do you think I care too much what people think? Because I think I've organized my personality wrong. My personality's not working. My personality's *so* not working. Like, should I just not care what people think and do the stuff I want to do and fuck them?"

"I'm not sure I understand what you mean. Fuck who?"

"Because I look at people who *are* successful and they're

all totally self-absorbed and focused and don't care what people think. Which I find to be kind of ridiculous but whatever, it's working for them. Meanwhile, I keep making decisions to change my life but nothing's really clicking. I mean I *know* I have to change something. I just don't know what it is yet."

"What would be something you'd like to change?"

"Where's that voice-over, you know? I keep waiting for that voice-over."

"Which voice-over?"

"You know. The voice-over that goes, 'For Twyla Bacsinszky, it was a week like any other. But little did she know, when she awoke that fateful Tuesday morning, that her life was about to change forever.' *That* voice-over. Where is it? Why am I trapped in the same old bullshit? Why am I always fucked up? I mean, I know there are patterns. 'Look at the patterns. Look at your choices.' I swear if I hear that one more time I'm going to shove a fork in my eye. But I have three fucking degrees, I speak six languages, I own my own condo. Why can't I do this?"

"I'm just wondering," says Dr. Symons, "when you have these thoughts all at once like this, what impact do they have on you? What sorts of feelings are you having? How do you feel right now?"

"Frustrated!"

"So these thoughts are –"

"It's just always the same," says Twyla. "I need a way to manage my fucked-up shit. And I think I thought by this time I'd be more grown-up. Everybody else my age is getting married and having families. And what am I doing? I'm sort of bopping around la-la-la dating multiple kinds of people and being depressed but – I don't know – I used to be a happy person. I did. I always had the most friends. At school. At camp. In university. And I used to think people who got depressed were just freaks who lost the brain chemistry lottery." Twyla looks suspiciously at her ankle boots, as if they might be to blame for everything that has gone wrong this week. "I guess things are different now. My friends are different now. They're all in this different phase of life now. Like, I saw my friend Sally –"

A high-pitched beeping sounds twice in Twyla's purse. "I should look at that," she says, reaching for it. "Could be about my dad." She takes out her smartphone and reads through a text.

"Everything all right?"

"Fine," says Twyla, texting a reply with both thumbs. "It's just my texting personality and my real-life personality are getting farther and farther apart. It's ridiculous. I could be in the worst premenstrual bite-the-head-off-a-squirrel mood possible and I get a text from work and I'm all smileys and exclamation marks. It's retarded."

"So it's from work?"

"No, it's from Justin."

"Right," says Dr. Symons. "When you spoke about your relationship being in limbo, did you mean your relationship with Justin?"

Twyla nods. "No one could possibly think about their relationship more than I do. I'm on the verge of insanity every minute of every day. I mean, I'm always afraid I'm not liking my boyfriend enough."

"You're always afraid?"

"Well, no, but we kind of had this big, huge fight." Twyla glances at Dr. Symons. "Basically he wants to have a baby and it's freaking me out."

"Do you?"

"I don't know. Usually I just get my period and don't care anymore. But relationships have to be over sometime, right? Or not." She sniffs. "We're supposed to go to a friend's wedding next week."

"Are you looking forward to that?"

"*God*, no. It's going to be disgusting. The bridesmaids are in these really dressy dresses with red velvet bows. It's just full-on retarded."

"I mean are you looking forward to going with Justin?"

Twyla shrugs. "I always think a million different things. I mean, I know I love Justin, but there's been some weirdness recently. I don't know –" Twyla makes a sudden sneer, as if to show that sifting through Justin-related complications might be too much for today's session, and checks the time on her smartphone.

Dr. Symons writes something in her notebook. "You said you saw your friend Sally."

"Sally Ogden-Byers," says Twyla, nodding. "This friend from Havergal. She's in town for the wedding and I ran into her at Whole Foods. She's just this disgusting, overly perfect Forest Hill person who I kind of hate. I don't really hate her?" Twyla puts her phone in her purse and places the purse on a nearby end table. "I just don't agree with the way she understands reality. I mean, Sally wins. She's winning the career game. She's winning the looks-exactly-like-she-did-in-high-school game. She's winning the life game. She's got the husband, the house, the picket fence. Whatever – fuck it – it just made me want to shoot myself in the head." Twyla smooths a kink in her skirt. "I mean I'm sort of over Toronto real estate gossip but they just sold their house in Cabbagetown – that her father basically *bought* for them – for two million dollars so they can move to Galiano Island. Because now Sally's all into sustainable biodiversity and ethical kale and I'm totally just like, 'Fuck off, murder me now, pardon me while I shrivel up with my desire to kill you.'" Twyla looks over at Dr. Symons. "So I ask how she's doing and she gives me this super-enlightened smile and says she's in such a good place in her soul right now and how this is a period of real discovery for her." Twyla turns to the side and makes a retching noise. "Ever notice how people who talk about their soul turn out to be the worst fucking pricks?"

"So seeing Sally again made you –"

"Seeing Sally again made me think why do the 'Be present, give space' thing when really I'm thinking 'Fuck this person,' you know? Because really it's sort of like, 'Oh, thank you, Sally, for your integrity and holistic outlook. It means so much to us still trapped in the commodified world that you would visit from your island dream home to participate in the world's inauthenticity.'" Twyla swings a hand dismissively toward the window. "And I just hate people who say 'Take care.' 'Take care.' It sounds so much like 'Fuck off.' It's sort of like '*I'm* not going to care about you so you better take care of yourself, idiot.' I know I'm sounding like the biggest bitch on the planet right now but I don't care. And I don't know why I hate her but I know it's the right thing to do."

Dr. Symons nods and glances at the clock on the end table. "You've said a lot today about your beliefs about yourself and your relations with others. And as you're talking, I can see it's bringing up a lot for you. But I'm also aware we're nearing the end of our session. So what do we want to take away from today?"

"Take away? What's the takeaway?" Twyla sighs. "How about I need a way to manage my fucked-up shit. How about I want to be in a happy relationship. Still going with that." Leaning to the side, so she appears again in the mirror, Twyla studies her reflection. "And if I don't cut all my hair off soon I'm going to kill myself."

"HELLO, I SUCK," says Twyla, swallowing a bite of chocolate and sweeping into the office. She drops her purse on the sofa, takes off her sunglasses, and faces Dr. Symons. "Once again? I suck." She sits in the middle of the sofa and flips her newly streaked hair. "This is my third Snickers in a row, by the way. I'm totally in fudge-the-pain-away mode.

But these?" Twyla holds up a Limited Edition Snickers Fudge bar. "These are super-legit. Just saying." She finishes the chocolate bar, crumples the wrapper, and tosses it into a nearby wastepaper basket. "When I crave chocolate like this it means I'm going to have a mega-period. I mean I'm seriously going to die if I don't start my period soon. And?" Twyla looks at Dr. Symons. "I fucking hate my family at the moment."

Sitting down in her chair, Dr. Symons opens her notebook. "You've said that before."

"I just came from Sunnybrook."

"Where your father's in the hospital. How is he?"

"He might have dementia. They're doing tests. But his new wife, Kewpie LaRoo – she's my age – I just can't deal. Tried to deal. But can't."

"Forgive me," says Dr. Symons. "You told me he's been married a number of times. But how many was it?"

"Just five. He must be doing something right. Or something wrong. You tell me. I went with my sister Ruthy and when we got there, there was a clusterfuck of ex-wives in the ICU."

"Was your mother there?"

Twyla quickly shakes her head. "Getting her nails done. Just the middle wives and Kewpie. But they got in this screaming match by the elevators about when to move him from intensive care. Yeah. Like it's *their* decision. That was pretty charming. It just made me want to cut off my family and move to Australia."

"Uh-huh? Where in Australia would you go?"

"Wait. That was a joke."

"Was it?"

"You want me to cut off my family?" Twyla makes a brief snort of disgust. "Well, why not? They've all fucking failed me. They all fucking suck. They're like this posse of emotional retards."

"What happens for you when you talk to them?"

"You know what Ruthy said when I told her I think Justin's an alcoholic?"

"What did she say?"

Twyla flutters her eyelashes and mimics her sister, "'You don't have to tell *me* about alcoholics, I've been married to three of them.'"

"And did you find that helpful?"

"Is that a joke? *No,* I didn't find that helpful. That's just Ruthy being a fucking bitch."

"How did you react when she said that?"

"I told her she was being a fucking bitch! Then you know what she says? She says it's because she and her husband haven't had sex in two years. I don't fucking blame him! How he fucked her once is a fucking mystery. I mean, when we lived in Côte Saint-Luc, Ruthy was the prettiest girl anyone –"

"Twyla, do you mind if we return to what we were talking about?"

"What were we talking about?"

"We were talking about what happens when you talk to your family."

"They're all fucking nuts. They're all fucking crazy." Twyla scowls. "I mean it's just so ridiculous that Ruthy would be like that. When she didn't come to my brunch for no reason – that pissed me off. But I said nothing. And when she asked me to pick up her kid from Tamakwa, I fucking did that, too, no questions asked." Twyla stares at Dr. Symons. "Don't I get anything?"

"So," says Dr. Symons quietly, "when you talk to your family, you're left with 'There's nothing for me here. I don't matter.'" She gazes at Twyla. "And what would you want?"

"For her to *listen* to me. Jesus." Twyla wipes at her eyelash. "And not be some self-obsessed jerk. I tried telling her what happened with me and Justin at the wedding – which is a whole other combo platter – and you know what she said? 'Well, why do you always go out with such sketchy guys?' And I thought, 'Could you maybe not assassinate my life choices at the moment?'" Twyla shuts her eyes, distressed. "She keeps de-self-esteeming me. I don't know. In Ruthy's brain, I'm this scabby alien sex addict. To Ruthy, I'm the Great Whore of Toronto. Ruthy just wants me to marry one of those guys in blue golf shirts and chinos you always see in airports. You know. Ted from Accounting."

Dr. Symons reads from her notebook. "So you went to the wedding with Justin?"

Twyla nods.

"How was that?"

"It was a lot of things. The good, the bad, the fugly."

"Shall we start with the good?"

"The good was the bride and groom actually loved each other. You could tell. They were like, 'You give me purity in my day.' 'Because of you, I dare to dream.'" Twyla smiles. "So of course all the other couples are immediately trying to act *as* much in love. It was bizarre. People arrive bitchy and exhausted from the drive but then it's like, 'Honey, can I get you another Prosecco?' And I like weddings but, fuck, the speeches drag on. This one old dude, it was like a dissertation on the Zohar. Anyway, after three hours of people pretending to be happy, I was *so* ready to explore the fullness of some perversion, you know. I told Justin we should go have sex on the golf course. Maybe try out hole number two. I don't know. We did the time. Might as well do the crime. But Justin so doesn't get the thread count."

"What does that mean?"

"It means he started behaving like a little fuck-boat and the worst dick-biscuit possible. I mean, we're at this beautiful resort for the weekend and all he wants to do is talk about the relationship?"

"Was this about having a child?"

"No," says Twyla. "Now he's not sure we should be together because he thinks I have a personality disorder." Twyla extends her middle fingers, waves them in the air, and addresses the wall. "*I* don't have a personality disorder, motherfucker." She turns to Dr. Symons. "He says I have narcissistic personality disorder. Do you think I have that? Is that my problem?"

"I'm not sure what someone else thinks you have is what we should be talking about."

"Does that mean yes?"

"No. It's just –" Dr. Symons leafs back in her notes. "Last week you said you wanted to find a way to manage your fucked-up shit. Do you remember saying that?"

"Sure. But –"

"Do you think recognizing what you're feeling would be useful toward doing that?"

"Toward managing my fucked-up shit? Yeah-duh. Obviously."

"I think it may be more helpful if you honestly identify your own reactions to events rather than worrying if you fit into the categories of a diagnosis someone else wants to label you with."

"Cool," says Twyla. "I can second that emotion. But here's a question. Why do I feel a need to grab a hammer and smash all his opinions back into his little pie-hole mouth?"

"That's a very good question. Why *do* you feel that?"

"Because I hate what he said to me! I'm like, 'Fuck you, Jack. Go solve your own life if you're so smart.'"

"I can agree with that," says Dr. Symons. "What feelings are coming up for you after that thought?"

"I don't know," says Twyla, uncertain. "This is weird. It's making me feel weird. I think I'd rather *be* my emotions than babysit them. I mean, I remember what you said about my behaviour impacting someone, but Justin's the one who lost his shit on the golf course."

"How did he do that?"

"By jumping up and down in a screaming rage and pushing a picnic table into a water trap."

"Has Justin ever threatened you?"

"Once he said I should be bitch-slapped down the stairs and locked in the basement. Does that count?"

"Did he ever hit you?"

"Not really. When we broke up two years ago I shoved him into a door and he backhand-slapped me."

"How often did that happen?"

"Just once."

"Has he ever shown you a weapon?"

"What's a weapon?"

"A knife, a firearm –"

"His father's got all that shit up in Muskoka. Why?" Restless, Twyla adjusts her sitting position with a hip wiggle. "Because, I have to tell you, this is kind of hot. Are you kidding me? Like, he's going to break in, all intense, in a ripped-up shirt, staring at me. Because I *love* it when he's Big Mad Daddy. It's fucking hot. I like the intensity of it. I like the tension. I don't know –" Twyla inhales deeply, her nostrils flaring. "My whole thing with Justin is we never know if we're going to fuck or not. Even if we're on a break. Because I know he still wants me. And he can't have me. But he still craves me. I can see it in his eyes. I fucking love it. Even if he's not looking at me, I can feel it. I mean, I totally know when he's thinking about me."

Dr. Symons writes in her notebook. "How were things left when you returned from the wedding?"

"I sort of slammed the car door when he dropped me off. So he'll ignore me for a while then send some late-night booty text like he always does."

"What will you do?"

"I don't know. Derp. I never know what I'm going to feel until I see him." Twyla looks at the clock on the end table. "Why? What do you think I should do?"

IN THE MIDDLE OF her fifth appointment, Twyla goes to the windows to investigate the blaring siren of an emergency vehicle. Two minutes later, long after the vehicle has vanished, she's still at the windows, standing there as if she can't decide what to do with herself. "I don't know," she says, pensive. "I sort of do this thing where, no matter what happens, positive or negative, I can always figure out some way I'm doing better than the other person. I can meet someone from high school and think, 'Sure, she has more money than me and she's got a house and a family, but is she happy? Because she looks pinched and her kids look snotty.' I mean, I could be in a room with Joe Biden and Gwyneth Paltrow and think *I'm* the one who's got it going on because I'm in touch with the street or whatever fucking lame-ass nonsense you want to throw down."

"That's called adaptive preference formation."

"Well, I'm the queen of adaptive preference formation."

"It's a way of reducing cognitive dissonance."

"I've heard of that. What is it?"

"It's when you have two contradictory ideas in your mind at the same time."

"Are you serious? That's my fucking *life*."

"Do you feel like that today?"

"Little bit."

"What are the two ideas?"

"I don't know. Magical thinking and blunt force depression."

"And," says Dr. Symons with a cautious smile, "which seems to be winning?"

"Well, it's been a weird day. It's been one of those days when I think if I fit into my Ultrasuede skirt and give money to a homeless person then everything will be all right. But it's not. I mean, I could barely get out of bed." Twyla crosses to the sofa and sits down. "I just feel like all the other times I was a failure was practice for this."

"So," says Dr. Symons, watching her. "You've felt depressed?"

"Yep. I mean, the good news is I lost twelve pounds. I look fucking great. I totally fit into that Ultrasuede skirt."

"How quickly did that happen?"

Twyla shrugs. "A week?"

"Losing twelve pounds in a week can be a shock to your system."

"So is breaking up a shock to your system."

"You broke up?" Dr. Symons looks up from her notebook. "With Justin?"

"He fucking *ghosted* me. You believe that? After five years, you don't fucking ghost someone."

"Does that mean you haven't heard from him?"

Nodding, Twyla lounges back on the sofa.

"Have you spoken to anyone else about it?"

"Oh, everybody's bored of me, Doc." Twyla rests her head on the sofa back and speaks to the ceiling. "I mean, to our friends, it's like me and Justin are trying to win the Come-Here-Go-Away Championship of Southern Ontario. They're tired of me complaining about my shit. They've heard it all so many times before."

"So how have you been dealing with this?"

"Vodka into oblivion."

Raising her eyebrows, as if to be sure she heard correctly, Dr Symon asks, "And how's that working for you?"

"Oh, look, I know I shouldn't binge drink." Twyla sits upright. "I mean, it's fun for a while. Then later – *yay* – I hate myself even more."

"What does that mean – binge drink?"

"Guys buy me drinks and I go with it."

"How many drinks would that be?"

"Maybe three or four. Or six or twelve."

"Are you concerned about how much you're drinking?"

Speaking in falsetto, Twyla says, "Bee-bee boo-boo." Then, in a more direct tone, she adds, "*Yes*, I'm concerned about how much I'm drinking. But come on. My relationship's fucked. What am I supposed to do?"

"And that's why you've been binge drinking?"

"Totally. And it's why I revenge fucked some random guy in a bar."

"To get back at Justin?"

"And I made sure he knew it, too."

"How did you do that?"

"I put it on Instagram. I posted a photo of me and this rando making out."

"With the man you met in the bar?"

"William. We met in one of those King Street bars where the girls are in short skirts and high heels and basically the tiniest outfits possible. This one bartender had the most ridiculous Friday-night hair I've ever seen. I mean she looked like a goddamn mermaid. Just the most back-combed, sluttarded bouffant updo possible."

"And this is where you met – you said his name was William?"

Twyla nods. "He's actually fucking awesome. Except he sort of has this weird-shaped head. But his *voice*. His voice drives me insane. It's like when you're getting your hair cut just before the hairdresser touches it. You know that feeling?" Twyla shivers. "Because, look, not going to lie, sometimes I need someone to pull my hair back and fuck me so hard I won't be able to walk the next day. I mean, who hasn't done that a million zillion times?"

Dr. Symons looks at Twyla, a little perplexed. "Do you like him?"

"Sort of. Except when we were having sex he said, 'Bounce your weight on me.' Which pissed me off. Bounce my weight on you? I just lost twelve pounds, bitch. And he called me Shyla. What the fuck is that? I only had your dick in my mouth till you came, motherfucker. And dude doesn't even remember my name? I mean I know I'm a sex addict but come *on*, people. At least I can remember a name." Twyla frowns at Dr. Symons. "Hey, I'm funny, God damn it."

"Twyla –"

"Ooh. Tough room."

"Do you mind if we return to what we were talking about?"

"Sure, but honestly I can't handle another lecture right now."

"What feels like a lecture?"

"Well, you don't really lecture. But your pauses interrogate me every week. And you don't have to ask me how that makes me feel because it makes me feel like I'm failing some fucking midterm. When you do your little pause thing, it's like it's obvious what everyone should think, so then I have this anxiety I'm going to get the wrong answer. But wait" – Twyla holds up a finger – "maybe my *anxiety's* the answer! You see, I'm learning. Double yay for me."

"Is this binge drinking" – Dr. Symons looks up at her – "something you feel you need to do for a while?"

"I don't really want to ask myself that question."

"And going out and meeting new men –"

"Yo, I did that *once*."

"Well, in terms of self-care, what have you been doing? Have you been going to sleep at the same time and –"

"Fuck, no," interrupts Twyla. "I'm all over the place. Last night I was online for six hours straight. After clicking on random shit like 'Twenty-Five Celebrities You Didn't Know Were Actually Ugly' it was on to 'Top Ten Signs You Might Have Narcissistic Personality Disorder: Number Nine Might Surprise You.' Well, number nine did more than surprise me. Number nine made me want to slit my own throat. Number nine made me want to go out and drink."

"And did you?"

"Nuh-uh. Stayed *home* and drank."

"You were drinking by yourself?"

Twyla nods. "I bought this bottle of red wine? Just took a chance on it and it was disgusting. Seriously. That shit was putrid. I was gagging right to the end of that bottle. So then it's three in the morning and I'm on the weird part of YouTube watching this four-year-old doing a puppet show for her gerbil. And I am literally sobbing. Just tears and crying and stabbing pains deep inside and it's like, 'Why am I crying? What's wrong with me? Why does this seem so important to me?'"

"Why did it seem so important to you?"

"Because it was real. It was pure. It was true. She loves her gerbil. I don't know –" Twyla shakes her head, helpless a moment. "Before Justin, I sort of went out with the Seven Dwarfs, you know? Sleazy. Skeezy. Drunkie. Whoever. What I mean is, I was just in all these weird, random relationships without ever being in love with the person. But Justin I care about. I do love him. I sort of *am* him.

We're the same person. And being away from him? I just feel so lonely. I miss him. I miss his man-stink. I miss his man-hands. I can't stand it. I don't know. I don't know. I think maybe I lost it somewhere along the way. In middle school, Sally Ogden-Byers came up to me at this birthday party and said I was weird. And I thought, 'Fuck you, Sally.' But now I don't know. I think maybe she was right. Maybe I *am* weird. Because everything I do becomes a disaster." She sighs. "Like I said, all the other times I was a failure was just practice for this."

"SO WE HAVEN'T SEEN each other for a while." Dr. Symons takes her notebook from her desk and sits in her chair. "We haven't seen each other in – what is it – three weeks?"

"Sorry I cancelled those appointments." Twyla moves to the sofa and chooses to sit, not in the middle, but at the far end. Today she wears an oversized sweatshirt and yoga pants, her hair in a ponytail. "I'm just sort of postponing everything."

"And this would be, I think, our last session?"

"I guess."

"You wanted to try six sessions to see if this was something you wished to continue with."

"Oh, right."

"And if it is, you can let me know."

"Yup."

Dr. Symons opens her notebook. "And how have the last three weeks been?"

"Well, my father's out of Sunnybrook. I can't remember when we talked, but the CT scan revealed he had two small strokes. So he doesn't have dementia. At least not yet. And he's talking again. Apparently you can retrain the brain. Rewire the pathways."

Dr. Symons nods, taking in this information. "They have a very good team at Sunnybrook."

"Totally true. So" – Twyla knocks twice on the end table – "good times there."

Dr. Symons looks alertly at Twyla. "And what about you?"

"Oh," says Twyla, "a little of Column A, little of Column B."

"Uh-huh?"

From Twyla's purse comes a high-pitched beeping. She takes out her smartphone but chooses not to look at the text. Instead she powers it off. "If I tell you something, you're not going to say things happen for a reason, right? Because whenever anyone says that, I always think about those guys on death row. What do they say? 'If I hadn't done the things I did then I wouldn't be where I am today.' Yeah, buddy. Which is on death fucking row."

"What did you want to tell me?"

"But *do* you think things happen for a reason? Like, it's all part of God's Plan? Or Nature's Way?"

"Maybe a way to think about it is that there are things in life we can't control. And things we can."

"Right. So I can't control some asshat cutting me off in traffic. But I can control how hard I smash my car into his.

Coolsies." Twyla leans down, picks a piece of lint from the Persian carpet, and flings it toward the wastepaper basket. "So this therapy," she says. "I don't know what I think of it. It's sort of making me confront the fact that even after thirty-four years on the planet, I still don't know why I do the stupid shit I do."

"Some people go their whole lives without knowing. This takes courage, Twyla."

"Yeah? I mean, I know I can be a megacritical negatron. I'm not really a glass-half-full person. I'm more a glass-half-empty-and-shatters-and-cuts-everyone's-face person. But I'm not a monster. I do have a heart."

"I think you've shown that here."

"But the last few days," says Twyla, a trifle distracted. "I've been feeling fucked up. Like just mood swings and hostility and depression. It's totally like, 'DJ, spin that shit.'"

"What's been happening to make your mood swing?"

"I don't know. Maybe it's because I know I should probably quit drinking. Maybe it's because I don't know if I *can* quit drinking. Or maybe it's because Justin sort of raped me."

"Oh, Twyla," says Dr. Symons softly. "Can you tell me what happened?"

"He held me down and had sex with me when I told him I didn't want to."

Dr. Symons closes her notebook and leans toward Twyla. "When did this happen?"

"Sunday."

"What was happening for you?"

"When he was sort of raping me?"

Dr. Symons nods.

"I don't know. It was just sex."

"Was it?"

"Well, I was sort of drunk."

"How drunk?"

"Not blackout drunk. But drunk. But maybe it's like –" Twyla shifts to a falsetto. "'Of all the girls in the world, he decided to rape *me*, you know? I'm special.' Nah. Lame joke."

"Twyla," says Dr. Symons. "You're allowed to take this seriously." She closely regards her. "Do you want to tell me what happened?"

"Well," says Twyla. "We went out to have a civilized conversation. I took him for dinner at this place we go. It's nice. We have a bottle of wine and la-la-la and I'm sort of thinking we'll go home and have crazy make-up sex, you know? But when we get to my place, in my bedroom, it was weird. Justin was weird. It was like the nice Justin was gone. The weird Justin had taken over. And then – and then –"

"Do you remember what you were thinking when it was happening?"

Twyla looks at the Persian carpet, her eyes unfocused. "That no one should know. That our friends shouldn't find out. That I shouldn't talk about it. Just get through it. Delete."

"What do you mean – delete?"

“Forget it. Move on.”

“Do you think it’s something that should be forgotten?”

“Well –” Twyla winces, her eyes filling with tears. “Actually, no.”

“Can you say that again?”

“No, it shouldn’t be forgotten. Because it’s fucked up what he did.”

“Yes, it is.”

“Because people should have sex because they love each other. Not because – not because they want to get back at me.” Twyla makes a pained smirk. “And I *hated* him for thinking he could do that to me.”

Dr. Symons continues to gaze at Twyla. “Anything else?”

“I felt messed up. And heartbroken and fucked up. And fucked over. And just putrid and disgusted and just – and just –” Twyla is searching for the right word when she abruptly lurches to the floor and grabs the wastepaper basket. Placing it under her mouth, she prepares to be sick. After multiple convulsions, during which her airway is blocked for some seconds, she finally sucks in a breath before her diaphragm contracts again. Then – following two more dry heaves – she spits into the wastepaper basket. Sniffling, she climbs back up on the sofa, her forehead moist with sweat, a delinquent smear of saliva on her chin. “I tried so hard with Justin,” she says. “And so much of the time I felt I was in heaven with him. But I know what this means.”

“What does this mean?”

"It means I have to forget him."

"It might mean that."

Twyla wrinkles her nose and whispers, "It just makes me so sad."

Dr. Symons offers Twyla a box of Kleenex. "Why are you sad?"

"Because I know it's over."

"What's over?"

"The relationship." Twyla takes a sheet of Kleenex. "But I sort of don't want it to be. I don't know. A part of me wants to hope it can still work, you know?" Wiping her chin with the Kleenex, Twyla looks past Dr. Symons, as if seeing some other scene entirely. "He was so sweet to me last summer in Montreal. I thought we were going to have the best life together. For one fricking nanosecond I thought maybe – *maybe* – I could be happy with someone for the rest of my life."

"I can hear the sadness in your voice –"

"Hey," says Twyla, dropping the wadded Kleenex in the wastepaper basket and glancing at the ring on Dr. Symons's left hand. "Can I ask you a personal question?"

"If you like."

"How many times have you been married?"

"Twice."

"And you kept your first husband's name?"

"I did."

"What does C. A. stand for?"

"Crystal-Ann."

Twyla stares at the Persian carpet, as if searching for new patterns in its design. "I never knew what the initials stood for."

"You can call me Chris if you want."

"You said we could go by first names. On the first day. But I was too shy." Twyla takes a deep breath and looks up at Dr. Symons. "Thank you, Chris, for listening to me. But here's another question –"

"What's that?"

"Am I crazy?"

"I don't think you're crazy."

"Do you think I'm a horrible person?"

"That's not what I think, Twyla."

"What do you think?"

"Do you remember what you said when you first came here?"

"What'd I say?"

"You said you wanted to be in a happy relationship."

"Oh, yeah. I said that."

"That's what I think. That's why I think you're here. And someone interested in that, I feel, is actually a good person."

Twyla's face twists with sudden sadness. "But I feel so shitty," she says. "I think I'm going out of my mind. I don't remember ever feeling this lost and insane before. And I don't think I can continue to live like this. I worry so much. I worry so much. I have so many fear-thoughts and I feel so helpless and out of control that I think I'm going to get some horrible – I don't even want to *name* it because then I'll get it – but like some disease or health problem because I'm so fucked up with panic and self-loathing and worry and anger." Twyla stares at Dr. Symons, warm tears spilling down her cheeks. "So you have to let me know, I'm fucking serious, is this going to be worth it?"

"Yes," says Dr. Symons firmly. "Or let me put that another way. Do you want it to be worth it?"

"Yes! Teach me how to do this. Show me how to live."

"I'm not sure another person can show you how to live. But you can learn it for yourself. Because the way you've been here, letting me see who you are and sharing how you're feeling, the fact that you can do this in here, it shows you can do the same thing" – Dr. Symons points at the windows – "out there. Do you want to do it?"

"*Yes*. For God's sake, please. I do. I do. I do."

Grace

"GET IN THE TRUCK!" said Wyatt, flipping through radio stations in the driver's seat of the pickup. "Let's do this. You want to grab that drink?"

But Tom, walking down the hill from the farmhouse, didn't appear to hear him. He was gazing into the February sky, watching the sunset flame inside a swirl of storm clouds. Tom wore a baseball cap, mackinaw jacket, caulk-spattered jeans, and untied workboots. Turning to look at a new housing development at the bottom of the hill, he asked, "How many beer did you have?"

"I don't know," said Wyatt. "Three, four? Nice of her to offer us beer. How many old ladies have beer in the fridge?"

"And you want to go to town? For what?"

"Maybe another beer and a whiff of lip gloss."

"Yeah?" said Tom. "Maybe another beer and a whiff of something else."

People in town weren't sure why Tom and Wyatt were friends. Maybe it was because the two simply liked to drink together. Or because Wyatt taught a teenage Tom how to drive stick. Or because Wyatt was one of the few people left alive who remembered Tom's father. Whatever it was, there was history between them and it was why, at certain times of the day, you might see Tom smiling at the older man, as he was smiling now, fondly contemplating the three coats Wyatt was wearing – which were a fleece hoodie, hockey jacket, and Ski-doo parka. The three coats had been worn together so much and so often they'd fused, in Tom's mind anyway, into one multi-layered Wyatt-related entity.

"You messing with a man's radio?" asked Tom, as if mystified. "You goddamn filthy animal. I don't need to hear your punk rock bullshit."

"Punk rock?" After checking through every song on every available radio station, Wyatt left it on "She's Not There" by the Zombies. "These songs, my friend, taught me how to live." He adjusted the treble. "How'd it go with the estimate?"

"I don't think it's for her."

"What number you quote her?"

"Twelve."

"Twelve? You say it in a nice-guy-trying-to-give-you-a-deal way or a take-it-or-leave-it-old-lady way?"

"Dude," said Tom, opening the passenger-side door, "I'm not going to worry about the right way to say shit."

From behind the seat, from a jumble of hard hats and bungee cords, Tom grabbed a large bottle of Scotch. It was about half full. He uncapped it, drank from the bottle, and offered it to Wyatt. "I gave her an estimate, I gave her an estimate. We don't really need the gig."

"But you said twelve grand?" Wyatt took the bottle. "She doesn't have twelve grand. That family doesn't have twelve grand."

"A roof lasts forty years. That place looks eighty. And I don't think they've ever replaced it."

"Not that big."

"Twenty-square roof. And with three-tab shingles, drip edge, underlays –"

"Doesn't need two layers of underlay. You quote her two?"

"She's got four dormers. They're fucking steep. And if she doesn't want some piss-poor job done, then yeah, it adds up. But fuck –" Tom looked again at the farmhouse. "Wyatt, it's not only the roof. You saw where the gutter leaked. And the basement flooded. That's foundation damage. That's a tear-down."

Wyatt nodded along to the offbeat drumming in the song. "I know what this is about," he said, "and it's not about the old lady."

"What's it about?"

"New Year's."

"New Year's what?"

"And that was ages ago."

Standing outside the pickup, Tom bent down so he could look through the cab at Wyatt. "So I should forget it?"

"Yes." Wyatt drank from the bottle of Scotch. "You should forget it." He leaned across the front seat and handed the bottle back. "Is that why you didn't go to Sully's birthday? Because Bryn was there?"

"She was there?" Tom rested the Scotch on the seat. "You see her?"

"Is that why you weren't there?"

"What – I'm supposed to be friends with her now? So she wins? No fucking way." Tom sniffed. "Who was she there with? You talk to her?"

"I like Bryn," said Wyatt, turning to stare out the windshield. "She's smart. Look, she's a bit of a wild child. Maybe she doesn't always know what she's doing and going out with her –"

"Was a fucking disaster."

"– would be like going out with a whirlwind."

"A messed-up alcoholic whirlwind. She's a fucking disturbed individual."

"She has some figuring out to do. She's struggling to –"

"She's struggling all right."

"But you two –" Wyatt turned down the radio to properly think through this next part. "I don't know. It looked like one of those we're-both-alive-at-this-moment-so-what-are-we-waiting-for type deals. So you went for it. Why not?"

"I more than fucking went for it."

"But it's not her mother's fault."

"Or," said Tom, "maybe it is."

"You take it out on Grace? Bryn's one person, her mother's another. What'd Grace ever do to you?"

Tom gazed at Wyatt, his head to one side. "Why are you being so fucking gay right now? You're having feelings, is that it?" Tom stood up straight, pushing his shoulders back, and took in a breath of chilled air. "I have no problem with Grace. And I don't want one either."

"So why gouge her on an estimate?"

Tom fished a pack of cigarettes out of his mackinaw jacket. "You fucking crack me up, old man. You really do. You can barely fucking walk, limping around, falling off ladders, but you crack me up."

"Are you getting in this truck?" Wyatt watched Tom light a cigarette. "Or are you going to stand out there and smoke?"

Putting his lighter back in his pocket, Tom dragged on the cigarette. "I've been with a lot of women. I've been with women I don't even remember their name. I'm serious. I'd be scared to say what I think their name is in case I get it wrong. But Bryn?"

Cocking his head, Wyatt said simply, "You loved her."

"She's somewhere between the sweetest girl in the world and a fucking psychopath."

"That's *all* women, Tom. All women."

"She tells me she cares about me? She says I can trust her? None of that shit was true. I couldn't even trust her to make a phone call. How did I go from being the best thing to happen to her to someone who doesn't rate a phone call? How the fuck?" Blowing a smoke ring into the air, Tom watched it fade away. "I couldn't believe it. I could not believe it." He glanced at Wyatt. "I knew we were broken up. I could fucking feel it. A month before Christmas, she's begging me not to give up on her. Remember that? And the whole fucking time she's freezing me out. Not returning calls. Voice mail full. How is it fucking full? But I knew what was going on."

"What was that?"

"She's dressing up hot and going out with her girlfriends –"

"Nothing wrong with looking good."

"It's more than that, dude. It's way more than that." Tom sucked on the cigarette. "Tequila shots and making out with her friend on the dance floor and doing coke with Percival till two in the morning? You're telling me that's not intentional? You're telling me she doesn't know what she's doing? She *knows* what she's doing. She's letting people know she's back on the market. She's out there with a fucking 'For Rent' sign around her neck, that's what she's doing. Of course some guy's going to come along." Tom looked at the burning end of his cigarette. "It's like when she shoplifted those earrings and walked out of the store with them on. Remember I told you that? You think she didn't know what she was doing? She did. She must've. And you know what she said when I told her to give them back? She's like, 'Well, they steal from the Earth.' Like it's some multimillion-dollar conglomerate raping the environment. It's not. It's

Tina Beaton trying to keep a jewellery store going in a mall in New Minas. Tina Beaton's not stealing from the earth."

"I can't speak to that, Tom."

"You can't speak to that?"

"I wasn't there."

Tom made a scornful sniff. "And you think Bryn's smart? Yeah, she's smart. Not brain smart. Not book smart. But pussy smart. Every email, every phone call, every text, she's playing you. Spinning your heart one way and your dick another. And she can string a guy along for days, weeks, years even. That's why so many guys think they have a shot with her. The only thing she has, the *only* thing she has, dude, is how hot she is. I mean, when I saw her that first time, I was dead. When you meet her that first time, and she's acting like some lovey-dovey high school girl, wearing lipstick and twisting her hair and you can't believe it's going to happen –"

"Don't forget that," said Wyatt, "because that moment's real –"

"Then when she gives it all to you?" Tom snapped his fingers. "She takes it away like that. And you're fucking dead again. I don't fucking know, Wyatt. I thought love would win the day. I didn't know it would lead to the most miserable fucking time of my life." Tom thumb-flicked the butt of his cigarette. "You remember what she said about her ex? That fucker Croydon? 'I think he knew I could replace him sooner than he could replace me.' That's what she said. I should've known she's going to be saying the exact same thing about me one day." Tom glared at the remains of the cigarette. "Sure. Replace me with somebody. A cop. A teacher. A drug dealer. Go find someone else to torture. I could give a fuck. But I don't. Not anymore." Tom flipped his cigarette into the driveway. "So fuck her and her mother. I'm done." Glancing into the darkened sunset, Tom walked around the truck to the driver's side. "Move over, chief. I'm driving."

Wyatt sat in the driver's seat, frowning at a crack in the windshield.

"Wyatt, you all right?"

"Yep." Wyatt slid out of the pickup truck. "Fine." He walked around the back of the truck. Staring at the Alberta licence plate, he kicked the mud off the words "Wild Rose Country."

Tom was watching him in the rearview mirror. "What're you doing?"

Wyatt continued around the pickup but he didn't move toward the opened passenger door. Instead, he walked into the driveway to collect Tom's still-burning cigarette.

"Wyatt. Dude. Get in the truck."

Twisting the cigarette in his fingers, Wyatt separated the burning ash from the filter. As the ash fell to the ground, he stomped on it, extinguishing it, then stashed the filter in the back pocket of his jeans.

"What are you doing, old man? You pooping out? You pooping out on me? Is that what you're doing? Pooping out?" Tom smiled. "Just get in the truck, all right? Let's bounce."

"I will," said Wyatt, "when you go up there with a proper quote."

Tom shook his head dramatically, as if responding to something wonderfully absurd, and his next words were spoken in a singsong falsetto. "*Fuck* off." He glanced at Wyatt. "Fuck that. I'll buy you whatever drinks you want. Get in."

Wyatt didn't move.

"You doing this? You actually doing this right now?" Tom turned the radio off and looked at Wyatt. "You want to get in the fucking truck, please?"

"I'm fine. I'll walk."

"You're going to walk twenty miles? That supposed to be funny? Because the way I see it, you're being a dick. Get in the truck."

"*I'm* being a dick?"

"How many beer did you have? You drunk?"

"Maybe."

"You're not getting in the fucking truck?" Tom reached over and pulled shut the passenger-side door. "Fine. Done. Gone." Tom turned the key in the ignition, fired the engine, and put the truck in gear. The tires spun wildly before finding purchase in the dirt. The pickup shot forward, lurched to a sudden stop, brake lights shining, then it started reversing toward Wyatt, tires sliding on the frosty grass. The truck slid to a stop with a fishtailing shudder, the back bumper knocking into Wyatt's knee.

Tom jerked out of the cab. From the truck bed, he grabbed a seventeen-inch wrecking bar. "Jesus Christ, you burn my ass, dude. Why? Why do you do it? Just fucking tell me."

Wyatt shrugged. "Everybody looks at the same sky."

"*What?*"

"Nothing."

"You're a freak, buddy! You really are. You are a strange, strange old man."

"Tell me something," said Wyatt, "why'd we come here? If you knew you didn't want the job, why'd we come here?"

Tom wiped his nose with his knuckle. He gazed at Wyatt. Then he flung the seventeen-inch wrecking bar back into the truck bed – it landed with a clang – and grabbed the bottle of Scotch from the cab. Leaning against the side of the truck, Tom brought the bottle to his lips. After a few swallows, he held the bottle in the air, offering it to Wyatt, who shook his head. "No?" said Tom. "Drunk enough already? Is it one of those drank-all-day-now-I-need-to-chill-type things? My Christ, who the fuck else would give you a job, buddy? Who the fuck else?" Tom noticed a rip of skin on the back of his thumb. "Bryn, yeah, so I got hung up on her and the bullshit of her everything. I did that. That was me. I admit it. I wanted it to work. Fuck, I wanted it to work."

"You sure it's over?"

"I waited six years to ask her out. Six fucking years. My mistake was taking it serious."

"Maybe."

"Dude, I know what I'm talking about. I was there. Whatever. Same old story. Her own bullshit will fuck her up in the end. Always does. Maybe it has already. You're friends with the new guy. Why don't you ask him?"

"I'm not friends with the new guy. When's the last time you saw them?"

"I don't want to see them. If I see them, I'm going to picture his dick in her mouth and I'll want to split his fucking head open."

"No, I don't think that lasted."

"How do you know that?"

"*Everybody* knows. In this town? Everyone knows everybody else's business."

"Everybody knows?" Tom watched as the rip on his thumb coloured with blood. "Then I got to get out of this place. I got to leave this redneck hick town."

"And go where? Back to Fort Mac?"

"Fort Mac?" Tom laughed. "Fuck that. Herpes and blow at fifty below? I've never been more fucked up."

"So where you going?"

"Out of my fucking mind." He looked at Wyatt. "You want to watch?" Tom made a mighty sigh. "Jesus fucking Christ, buddy. The things I do for you." He finished the last of the Scotch and hurled the empty bottle down the hillside. It bounced along the dirt and clanked into one of the exposed culverts of the housing development. Tom stared at it a moment, then he wiped his bleeding thumb on the sleeve of his mackinaw jacket and started up the hill to the farmhouse, the heel of his left foot, in his untied workboot, slipping up and down with each step.

20 Herring Cove

DO YOU GUYS MIND if I sit here? Because this is kind of a real thing. See that guy? That guy's been staring at me since the whole time I got on the bus. That man. And now he's coming over? He's coming over! Just keep talking. Keep talking like you know me. Pretend you're telling me a joke and I'll laugh. Just anything. Ha! Like that. "Hilarious! Oh, God, you guys, too funny –" Okay. He's getting off. He's getting off. No, he isn't. He's still there. But he's sitting down. What is he doing? Is he picking his nose? Holy fucking purple Jesus. Like, what is even going on right now? Because I'm going insane. I really am. I'm not even kidding. I swear to God, I'm mentally brain damaged.

Hi, I'm Crystal. You can call me Chris. I sit behind you in Biology. But I'm wearing my contacts today so no one recognizes me anymore. You wouldn't believe the people who walk by me now. My mom. My dad. My cat. Not my cat but you know what I mean. And you're friends with Donny and Deedee, right? That's where I've seen you before. I love Deedee. I mean you can meet somebody and hang out with them five years, never see them again, and not think twice about it. Somebody else, you meet them and you know you're going to be friends forever. Like Deedee. She's so funny! You don't even have to think of any jokes or put-downs or anything. You just start laughing. We hung around all through elementary. We probably spent every single recess together in the girls' bathroom in grade six. And now she's going to have this crazy humongous giant party. You hear about it? You should totally go. But I don't know if I'm actually a hundred per cent going yet? I know, I know. If I don't go, I'll wish I should've came but I don't know if I actually can because I'm sort of grounded. Maybe I'll go. I don't know. Depends on my crazy mother. Or my crazy father –

Whoa! Did you see that? That fucking snowball almost broke the back window! Who threw it? Fucking Jason. Go fuck yourself, Jason! Because even if he threw it as a joke he still did it and that's weird. Fucking Jason. He's a funny kind of little I-don't-know-what. Everyone's so in love with him, you have to admit he's cute, obviously, and there's always this obscene amount of girls in love with him, but I don't know. We went out for two and a half months and then he's like, "Let's see each other without a label. I don't want to label it." Which kind of means "I'm going to get with other girls and you can suck it" is what it means. But I couldn't really see myself staying with him forever anyway. Personality-wise, it wasn't going to work. People either grow up or stay the same, you know? Doesn't matter how hot you are. Doesn't matter how cute you are. And he's the exact same as he was in grade nine. Exact same. Like last New Year's was so gross! I got locked out of my house and had to go to Jason's to call my mother and his girlfriend's in the next room passed out and you know it's New Year's so he totally tries to stick his tongue down my throat. And I'm just like, no. Barf. Suck. Garbage. Jason can be a walking pile of garbage. Because personally I know for a fact you do not try and stick your tongue down someone's throat if you're going out with someone. You don't. Plus a ton more other disgusting stuff. There's like all this other weird shit that happened, I can't even talk about it, that's like forbidden ground. I'll tell you later. Tell you later. But if you knew? You would barf. You would. You would seriously barf. Fucking Jason. He always says he's going to change but it never happens. Ever ever ever.

I mean I like a guy who's down to earth and you can talk to as a friend. But I'm very picky when it comes to relationships? Like my last boyfriend, he was this older guy that I was friends with, a real guy's guy, but I don't know. He was sort of boring or something. Maybe Deedee's right. White guys are overrated. So, yeah, no, I haven't exactly found my soulmate. And there's only one for each of us, right? Or is there? But maybe mine was born in Afghanistan or someplace. Like what if I my soulmate's in Afghanistan and got blown up? How would I know? Seriously, how would I know?

Oh, are you getting out here? Is this where you get off? Oh, for a second I thought you were getting off. Me? I have so far to go. I'm like way past the shopping centre. Way past the McDonald's. If you know where the lightning hit the Sobeys, then I sort of live behind that. But I don't even know where I'm living right now. Because like this month I was living with my mother, right? But my mother, it's not like I don't like her, I do, but I don't care if I ever see her again. She needs to fucking chill. I should probably not even talk to her anymore. Like my mother? She definitely for sure has some kind of serious mental problem. I don't know what it is yet but believe me it's there. Because she isn't normal! She isn't. And I don't think she will ever be normal. She always has to understand things her way, right? She never understands stuff like a normal person. She wants everybody to be the same as her and I'm just so fucking sick and tired of it. My mother freaks the fuck out all over me for no fucking reason and I don't want to be messed with anymore. I literally can't handle being with her for one more goddamn fucking day. Like I love my family, but my family's weird. I don't know in what way exactly they're weird? But they are. Trust me. Like, I know family's important and I love my mom and my aunt but there is no way – just no way – I could ever talk to them about anything real in my life. They wouldn't get it. They have no way of understanding it. It's so totally what's-wrong-with-this-picture, you know? Because my mother and my aunt, they live in a land of make-believe. Pretending their life is okay. Pretending their marriage is okay. Pretending they still have sex with their boyfriends. That's bitchy to say but it's true. I don't even try anymore. Because they're at this point now where they just totally believe their own lies. I'm serious. They're all brainwashed idiots who totally believe their own lies. Or they don't even know anymore that they're lying. That's what I can't believe. I swear to God you have no idea. Whatever. This is some weird shit, man. Like be whatever you want but don't fucking drag me into it, right?

And this guy's coming back? And – oh my God – can you believe this? Ew. Ew. *Ew.* I'm not even sitting down anymore. Hey! You fucking disgusting pervert! Yeah, you. Get the fuck off this bus. Get the fuck off. And maybe kill yourself while you're at it. What're you even waiting for? And, buddy? I've seen bigger. I've seen bigger!

Holy Jesus fuck hole. What is *with* people today? That guy is an excuse against humanity. I mean this is all probably hilarious in some other world but I swear to God, I've lost my faith in people. I really have. Who would *do* that? Why would a grown man expose his penis to a public bus? Why? I swear, if there's a weirdo on a bus? *Zoom.* Right over to me. Every time. But you just got to laugh, right? Or scream. Or buy a machine gun. Isn't that terrible? I knew it was going to happen, though. I could feel it. What the fuck is everyone's problem? I mean basically right now what I think is – like the main most important thing right now – is for all freaks to die as quickly as possible. It's just that there's a million thousand triple billion freaks in the world. Don't you think? Back me up on this. Fuck, I'll tell you, if there's a ticket to Mars, I'm on it. I'm out of here.

I like your perfume. What is it? Rosewater? It's kind of like that purple gum. I can't remember the name. It'll come to me. Do you know that gum? It's like purple Chiclets. It tastes like flowers or soap or something. Like, why is that even a candy? Could anyone please tell me? You know the gum I mean? Like when I was little I didn't know if it was a medicine or a candy. If it was like a Vick's cough drop or a Halls or what. It's in that little package and you look at it and you just *know* the same gum's been there for three years in the store because no one's boughten it. Like seriously what people *do* get that gum? I seriously think no one really buys that gum and they just put out the same packs year after year hoping somebody from Czechoslovakia will buy it because they don't know any better. I'm not even kidding.

What're you studying – Biology? Oh, right. That test. Actually I'm not doing that great in Biology anymore. I'm probably flunking out of everything but Drama and English. They're my favourite subjects. But I'm not even doing that great in English anymore. When I was in grade seven, I was doing like grade eleven English? And if I had an oral presentation due the next day, I wouldn't do it till the morning and I'd still get eighty-six. Like in my old school, it was so slack. And I was a great skipper, right? All you'd need is a note. They'd never check. They'd never call your parents.

I'd never be in class. And my old school was right next to a mall. And not a 7-Eleven or something but a real mall with shoe stores and everything. So we'd go hang out and steal something from Zellers, right? Oh! See that Mercedes? Dude. That's totally the kind of Mercedes I'd get.

My father, he has a red Lincoln. That's who's picking me up. At the end of the line. Or one stop before the end. I just pray to Jesus he isn't drunk. Ha! No, seriously, he could be. I don't know. It could be worse. I could still be with my mother! But I can't live with her another fucking minute which is why I'm going to live with my father now. I mean my father, he's bipolar, but at least he's sane. But my father, he has like this wedge or something with other people – I can't explain it – and it's in between him and everybody else in the world. And he can't get out of it. It's like in this circle and he can't get out of the circle. Or he can't join the circle together. I don't know. I'm not the greatest explainer in the world. But he has a really bad temper. My dad has a seriously bad temper. I mean my parents, they got married when they were seventeen, right? That's like two years from now. Is that crazy? My grandfather probably made them get married. He was so strict. But I am glad they split up. Believe me. It's way better my folks got divorced.

And my dad's girlfriend now, she's nice, she's this woman you've never heard of, but I have to watch everything I say around her. I mean it. I have to fucking watch *every* word I say around her. I mean, she's pregnant, right?

But she doesn't know if she wants to marry my dad anymore. They live in this one-bedroom apartment and – don't say anything – but I'm staying on the pullout sofa for now. We're supposed to be moving but maybe we won't all move in together. Because my stepmother? I mean it's basically fucking disgusting what her life is. She's just basically a piece of meat. She never went to school. She can't even work the VCR so she made me get the TV from the living room and totally disconnect it and everything and put it into their bedroom so she could watch this show except she was so shit-face drunk by then she didn't even know her show was over. And last Christmas? All they did was drink. I think they were going through a weird time and maybe broke up and got back together. I don't know. But it's fucking scary when they're both drunk. And my dad, if he's drinking, anything can happen, believe me.

But with my father and her, they make me work so hard. I have to do everything. They make me responsible for everything. Like I have a curfew. I never have any money. It's pathetic. I wanted to get a job but now with this kid I'm probably going to have to come home from school and take care of it. And I mean I already have a sister. My real sister, I haven't seen her in so long, she's really creative artistically. She got all nineties in school. She played the flute. But she moved out of the house when I was three years old. So she was like sixteen. And now? Don't know where she lives. Don't know where she is. It's like she disappeared off the face of the earth. I mean that's pretty fucked up. Even for my family.

Well, this is me. This is my stop. And don't worry, someday I won't hate everybody in the world. I know it's going to happen. I just don't know when! But you guys have been so nice. You listened to me, you saved me from the pervert guy, you've totally upholded my faith in humanity. See you Monday. Or talk to you later. My voice sounds really weird on the phone so don't worry. And if you see Donny in his Nova, tell him I said hi. He won't remember me and everything and then he'll go, "Who? Oh – oh, yeah. Crystal." Because I don't have glasses anymore and – Thrills! That's it. That's the gum I was trying to remember. Thrills. Snowballs. Perverts. Yeah, it's been real. And is that my dad? Yeah. That's my dad's Lincoln. Wait. He's turning around. But I think that's him. Yeah. That's him. I'm pretty sure that's him.

Turnaround

THERE ARE OVER six hundred industry people in the Hyatt Regency now that the film festival's begun but the couple in room 802 have been in Toronto since June when Hannah's cable series started principal photography. She dozes in bed amid sections of the Sunday *New York Times*, a MacBook Pro, and a full double pink draft of the series' final episode. Across from the bed, on the low-rise dresser, is a vase of sagging roses, wrinkled clumps of Canadian and American bills, and a manuscript, three inches high, serenely situated on a FedEx packet.

Sounds of plumbing – a flushing toilet, a running tap – begin in the bathroom, somewhat obscuring the noise of a briefly ringing cell phone, which is why, in the next moment, Brendan comes out of the bathroom to ask, "Is that someone's cell?" He wears a fluffy hotel bathrobe, at least two sizes too small, the sleeves extending only to his elbows.

"I thought I heard ringing." Instead of going to either of the cell phones, he takes a large cinnamon bun from the bedside table and grabs the *Times Magazine* off the bedspread.

He sits at the foot of the bed and skims an article about child soldiers in Sudan. Then, finding a Sharpie on the floor, he flips to the crossword puzzle in the magazine's back pages. As he begins printing in the first squares of the crossword, Hannah twitches once, twice, then jiggles her foot into the small of his back.

"Ah," says Brendan, "she awakes. Five letters for 'Too devout.'"

"Mmf."

"Starts with p."

Hannah speaks into a pillow. "Proud?"

"Tried that. Didn't work. 'Too devout.'"

"Too hungover."

"Come on, Cookie."

She opens one eye. "Pious."

"Yes! That's why I go out with you."

"No, you go out with me because I'm cute."

"Cute?" He considers her shape within the bedcovers. "You're gorgeous. Those pants last night were so sexy –"

"I know. I had to cut the bum out of my underwear so I wouldn't have panty lines. I don't have any more clean thong underwear. Can you believe that?"

"That's preposterous. That's an outrage. What kind of film festival is this?" Brendan smiles at Hannah, admiring how her hair splashes across a pillow. "Cookie, you did look beautiful last night, by the way."

"I'm just glad I'm finally known for what I do, not how I look."

"Exactly." Setting aside the marker and magazine, Brendan gets into a push-up position above her. "You can't help it if you're gorgeous." He bounces his pelvis into the underside of her thigh.

"No humping!" she says. "Too hungover."

"That's not what you said last night."

"Sweetie, I don't have a sexy bone in my body right now."

"That's where I come in." After a pause, he tilts his head. "Hey, that was pretty good."

"That was pretty good," says Hannah, quickly slipping a hand between her legs. "Wow. Itchy!"

"Why? What's the matter?"

Hannah flips over on her back, pushes away the bedsheets, and pulls up the lace-lined edge of her slip. "Whoof," she says. "Sorry, bud. Fifi's closed today."

"'Fifi's closed today.' Where'd we get that? Didn't someone actually say that?"

"Holy Toledo." Hannah examines herself. "Fifi's not looking so hot." She scratches two fingers through the line of her pubic hair. "I got big trouble in little vagina. Time for a wax. It's Sherman Forest."

"Sher*wood* Forest."

"Him too."

Brendan picks up the *Times* Magazine. Then he grabs

the cinnamon bun and takes a first bite. "Okay, then, help me with this. Five down."

"No idea. No clue."

"Let me *tell* you the clue."

"Hey –" She sits up, her face creased from the bedsheets. "That smells good."

He moves the cinnamon bun away from the bed. "Not a chance, kid."

"One bite?"

"I offered to order you one but you didn't want any."

"I didn't know it was going to be that good. Please?"

After a quick shake of his head, Brendan passes the pastry to her. "All right, Cookie DeLuca. Seven letters. Ends in r. 'Brief gleam' is the clue."

But Hannah has become interested in a blemish on the back of Brendan's neck. "Uh-oh." She puts down the cinnamon bun. Getting up on her knees, she deftly closes in with two thumbnails and pinches at the skin under his ear.

"*Ow!*" he says, in real pain. "What the hell are you doing?"

"I just – Don't move, okay?"

"What *is* that?"

"It's sort of a pimple. It looks like an infected hair or something but –"

"Just take a razor and hack it off."

"I tried but it's not going to pop. There's some blood. You might want to get a Band-Aid."

"A Band-Aid? I'm not going to be one of those guys who

walks around with a *Band*-Aid. People will think I've had a biopsy." Brendan stands up, his fluffy robe falling open, the belt ends dangling. He tosses the marker and magazine on the bed. "I can't get 'brief gleam.'" He glances at her. "Are we going to this gala tonight? Who's going to be there?"

"Errol said he might go. That's what he said last night."

"I didn't know you were talking to Errol. Working those pants, were you?"

"And there's a press screening for Gareth's movie."

"People are *going* to that? To a press screening? What kind of film festival is this?"

"I was looking at Gareth last night," says Hannah, licking the icing from her fingertips. "He's just so confident and cute. You can tell he was always like that. Way before he was a movie star."

"Gareth Trotter is not a movie star." Brendan examines his reflection in the mirror on the bathroom door, checking the back of his neck for blood. "Has he looked at his paycheque? That'll tell him if he's a movie star. Gareth Trotter is a television actor." He takes a bottle of Visine from the bedside table. "You talk to Errol? What'd he say?"

"He's here because he wants to make another movie."

"He's here because he *has* to make another movie." Angling his face toward the ceiling, Brendan squirts a few drops of Visine into his opened eyes. "You don't know this, but Errol has to make a movie or his deal expires with the studio. He's got forty million left in his envelope. That's why he's here."

"Did you tell him your idea for 'Romeo and Juliet' in a retirement home? I was telling Gareth about it. He thought it was gold."

"Cookie," says Brendan, blinking away the excess Visine from his eyelashes, "no one can know that idea." He turns to her, stern. "Things I tell you in private, I tell you in private."

"Sorry. But don't big-deal me, okay? I forgot so I forgot, all right?"

"Who else did you mention it to?"

"No one! If it's such an issue, don't tell me stuff I'm not allowed to know." Her eyes at that moment are radiantly open and evident on her face, just below her cheekbone, is a small circular hollow in her skin. It might be the result of any number of things – the residue of teenage acne, a birthmark, a scar left by the surgical removal of a mole – and when Brendan first became aware of it, six years ago, when Hannah was living as a law student in an East Village walk-up, he felt a rush of love so pure he hoped the feeling would stay inside him forever.

"I won't talk about your projects again," she is saying. "I promise. I love you. You know that. I'll make it up to you. I'll find a way."

"Or Fifi will."

"Oh, I'm sure she'll *have* to." Hannah bounces on the bed, as if it were a trampoline, leaps to the floor, and walks into the bathroom. "Oh," she says, lifting her slip as she sits on the toilet. "You know who I liked last night? Your friend Margo. She was like a normal person who doesn't care about the business."

"Margo's good people. She's a doctor." Brendan points at the manuscript on the dresser. "She just wrote a book about her year with a marine biologist. A memoir. She married him."

"Small world," says Hannah, returning from the bathroom, the sound of the flushing toilet fading behind her. "Is it good?"

"To be honest, it's not that good a book but it might make a brilliant fucking movie. The story it *wants* to be? I'd make that movie. They were sailing off Cape Breton when the guy had a heart attack."

"Huh. There's a honeymoon you don't forget. She have a publisher?"

"She's shopping it. No one knows about it."

Hannah is nodding when she abruptly turns to him. "Who was Errol's date last night? And what was she wearing? Some acrylic doily dress?"

"Now, now. There's no need to stoop –"

"Because she looked incredibly *un*sexy. Like something out of 'Dancing with the Stars Bulgaria.' Someone should tell her skunk streaks are over. She did look kind of familiar, though. Didn't she used to be your – what-do-you-call-it – wife?"

"Ex-wife, Cookie. And that was many years ago."

"And now you work with Errol. Anyone else find that weird?"

"Believe me" – he waves his hand carelessly – "I don't think about it. And neither should you."

"It's just sometimes – *fuck*." Hannah stares at a discoloured spot on the carpet. "Men have all the power in this world."

"And women," he says, moving to kiss the back of her neck, "have all the power over men's hearts."

"Over their dicks, you mean," says Hannah, evading him by stepping toward the dresser. She is rummaging for her cell phone when she suddenly slaps a hand on the dresser top. A single rose petal falls to the carpet. "God, sometimes I feel like this thing that gets passed around. Like that's all women are. This thing that gets passed around to facilitate the real relationships in the world. The ones between men." She picks up her phone.

"Cookie," Brendan says softly, "I thought we weren't going to check messages."

"I'm just seeing something." Pressing a button, Hannah raises the phone to her ear and listens. "There's a message here from Errol."

"What's he say?"

"He wants to know if we're going to the gala tonight. He says he'll call you. And – oh my God." She turns to stare at Brendan, completely absorbed in what she is hearing. "Oh my *God*."

"What are you oh-my-God-ing about?"

"Brendan," she says, "you have to hear this message. It's repulsive."

"Who is it?"

"Peter Svboda. Who else? He is possibly the stupidest man alive. God, he's an idiot. This is the third crazy message in two days. He thinks everything's a crisis. 'It's not too late to save the series.'"

Brendan watches her, waiting for what's coming next.

"Peter Svboda," she says, "doesn't like the cut of the pilot. He thinks the network's going to hate it because we didn't address their notes. He left a message for Nikki and he's already got the editor out of bed. He's going to turn this into some political shitstorm, I can tell. He wants me to call him back."

"Wait till Monday."

"He wants me to call him now."

"I wouldn't."

"I know what he's doing." She frowns. "This is some psychological ploy. This is his way of saving the series, you watch. He's going to side with the network because he wants to sell them his other show. That's what he's doing. But he's not getting final say on the pilot."

"Final cut."

"On *my* show? No fucking way. Fine for him to say everyone should work together. I'm the one doing sixteen-hour days in Bumfuck, Ontario. If just once – *once* – he said he was happy with the series. The scripts. A promo. Anything."

"Hannah?" Brendan sits on the bed and leans against the headboard, his bathrobe falling open. "These are very good problems to have. In two years you've brought a series from concept to production. Even better, the network's behind it. But the other night at dinner, the execs are hearing about episodes you guys are writing – but they haven't even seen outlines for – and they freak out. They can't just give you a pile of money and hope you show up with twenty-two episodes. They want to feel like they're involved. The writers to them – you guys were very cliquey the other night, laughing at jokes they didn't get, so they're feeling left out of their own production. So this is when you have to listen to them."

"I'm listening."

"And if they have an idea, put it in an episode and make them know it's there. Make them think they saved the episode with that idea. You want the confidence of the network right now. That's what Peter Svboda's finessing. And after a while they'll relax and stop paying so much attention and season two you won't get any notes at all."

"But how will we even *get* a season two if Peter Svboda is sabotaging us at every turn? And the idea of him *talking* to the network? He says stuff just to have an idea and assert his authority and it makes everyone incredibly tense because no one wants to challenge him even though his ideas usually turn out to be wrong because he doesn't have a clue what he's doing! And I can feel how much he wants it and how his insecurity is mixed up with all this jerk-off arrogance and it makes me crazy. There's something about him that you just want to *crush*." Hannah kicks at the fallen rose petal. "I'm calling him to tell him what an asshole he is."

Brendan holds up a hand. "You have to work with him for the rest of the season. That's three more months. And don't you have a feature in development with this guy? What do you think's going to happen there if your relationship falls apart? Getting emotional doesn't help. It just makes you look unstable. Hannah, ten minutes ago you were lying in bed eating a cinnamon bun and now you're bouncing off the walls like a lunatic."

"Because of Peter Fuck-Face! Brendan, you *have* to hear this message –"

"This is how he operates. He thrives on paranoia and crisis."

"I know! He creates his own pathology in everybody else so they're the idiot. So he's destabilizing everyone so he can live inside his own fucked-up behaviour."

"And if he makes everyone as panicked and dysfunctional as he is, he wins."

"Brendan –" Hannah speaks now in a defeated tone, as if something inside her has already broken. "I can't tell you how exhausting it is. All the infighting. And the idea the network might think Peter Svboda is *saving* the series? It makes me insane." She shivers. "He's such a miserable little weasel, I can't stand it. Being in the same room with him makes me sick. He's like a little sniffling rodent trying to get inside the cookie jar." Picking up her cell phone, she inspects it a moment, then tosses it on the bed. "My battery's dead. Where's your phone?" She grabs Brendan's cell phone from the bedside table. She has almost finished dialing when he gets off the bed and takes it from her.

"Cookie," he says, "Peter Svboda's an asshole. Everybody knows he's an asshole. But calling him on Sunday morning –"

"I'll call Nikki."

"You can do that. But what good's it going to do?"

"I want her to know what I have to work with every fucking day!"

"You don't think she knows? She knows. And you don't have to worry about guys like Peter Svboda. These guys self-destruct on their own."

"Oh yeah?" She grabs the phone from him. "How do I speed up the process?"

"Look, what's the most important thing here? What do you want to happen? Because there'll come a day when you aren't working with Peter Svboda anymore."

"When's that day going to come? Fuck, Brendan, you don't understand. I drop out of law school, *he* drops out of law school. I want to be a writer, *he* wants to be a writer. I become a producer, *he* becomes a producer. This man has been haunting me for seven years! So what I want to happen" – she inhales deeply through her nose, yoga-style – "is that Paramount greenlights our feature, I win an Oscar, and Peter Svboda ends up bankrupt, teaching media arts in a community college in Iowa. That's what I want to happen.

Because, Brendan?" Still holding the cell phone, she folds her arms across her chest. "I want to win."

"You've won already. You're sane. Look, it can be really depressing to see how this business works but you just have to treat this guy like a special needs person."

"Why should I have to treat him like a special needs person? That's what I can't abide. Why should I pretend someone's okay if I think they're fucked up? You have this illusion that being nice will make you successful but it's not true. It's no guarantee of anything because being nice in this business is a liability. Especially for a woman. And assholes like Peter Svboda are very successful. Because – I don't know, Brendan – I think the asshole always lives. The asshole gets drunk. The asshole smashes his car into the minivan. The nice family dies. The asshole always lives. That's what I think." She raises the cell phone over her head, defiant. "I'm calling him." But before she can make another move, the phone begins ringing in her hand. Startled, she reads the call display. Then she composes her face into a smile and takes the call. "Errol!" she says. "Just waking up?"

Brendan studies her.

"I know, I know," says Hannah, "I thought after the Jäger shots you were going to start table dancing." As she listens, Hannah begins nodding, her face frozen in a professional smile. "The gala tonight? Um, let me see if I can find Brendan. One second." Holding the phone behind her back, she looks to Brendan and mouths the words, "Are we going?"

Brendan shrugs.

Hannah brings the phone to her cheek. "Hey, doll. Can he call you back? Or can you call back in ten minutes?" She listens. "I'll be sure to tell him. Bye!" Without looking up, without risking any further distraction, she dials a new number. "Peter?" She sniffs. "You want to tell me what's up with all the messages?" Her eyes widen in disbelief. "Right. But it wasn't ready, Peter. No, it wasn't. Because it wasn't a locked cut, that's why. We discussed this on Friday. That was the director's pass. I hadn't signed off on it. Nikki hadn't signed off on it. You knew that. But then you sort of arbitrarily decide to call the editors out of bed and God knows –" She is halted by a strident eruption of conversation that is audible even to Brendan five feet away. "Okay, fine," she says. "Amazing. How about I tell *you* something?" She stares at the rose petal on the carpet, her mouth set in a fixed smirk. "Sure, sure. What's more important? There's always something more important –" Hannah goes still, the colour draining from her face. "No way," she whispers. She ends the call and drops to a sitting position on the bed.

After a moment, Brendan asks, "Are you okay?"

Hannah turns to the curtained windows with a peculiar half smile. "We got dumped."

"Who did?"

"Paramount's passing. They're putting my movie in turnaround. They develop my movie for four years and now they're dumping it."

"They put you in turnaround? Why?"

She stares vaguely at the curtains. "They say the script is lacking creatively. The script that everyone loves, they say is bad." Her fingers tighten around the cell phone. "I want to throw a rock through their fucking Range Rovers!" Abruptly, with a sneering smile, she flings the cell phone against the wall. It makes a gash in the drywall and clatters to the floor.

"Hannah?" Brendan looks at her, his head to one side. "Are you okay?"

"Would you stop *asking* me that?" Her look to him is full of irritation. "That was four years of my life! To come this far only to get dumped?" She falls backwards on the bed and gazes at the ceiling. "I can't believe how – I can't believe it."

"Well, think about Errol. He had a finished movie taken from –"

"I'm *not* Errol!" Hannah bolts upright, her voice sharp. "I don't care about Errol! I'm not Errol or Gareth. I'm me. And I have to stand up for myself and fight for what *I* believe in. Fine for Errol, he's got his name on eight fucking features –"

"Would you stop being so angry, Hannah. Please?"

"If you stop being like my teacher, all right? I don't care if you want to tell me something, Brendan. Or ad*vise* me. Just don't be a sanctimonious prick about it. You always act like you know the way things are going to go but maybe you don't. Maybe you're the guy who says everything's fine when nothing's fine."

"Hannah, you're behaving like –"

"And stop guilting me! I have to tell you something. I have to tell you something, Brendan. Can I say something? I'm just going to say this because otherwise I'm going to go out of my fucking *mind*. I mean, I know you've been patient while I've been a bitch on this series but sometimes you have this fiction in your head that I'm this reckless little go-getter and I'm getting more than a little tired of it. Because every time I get the least bit emotional you try to take the piss out of me and shut me down. And if you keep doing it, I swear, I will drop you out of my life. Because sometimes I just have to be angry and no amount of rationalizing is going to help."

"I'm not talking about rationalizing, Hannah. I'm talking about making the right decisions so you can put together a career."

"But that's not what happens! The way you say it, everything always sort of makes sense because you figure out some way to be right. But then I think, 'What's this guy done lately? Why isn't he up onstage getting the award?'"

"Okay. Maybe. But I'm not going to lie to people or fuck them over." Brendan re-belts his bathrobe. "Because the way I treat people is creating the way I can expect to be treated back. And I don't want to make that many enemies."

"Maybe a person afraid of making enemies is a person afraid of life. I don't know. I don't know if I care if everybody likes me, Brendan. I mean, I know what you're saying is true, I do, but sometimes you just have to say fuck it and go your own way, you know? Is it fair? No. Is it reality? Yes."

"I don't think it's worth the long-term bad karma."

"Which is why nine years after your only movie you're still pissing into your crosswords." She raises a hand, repentant. "I'm sorry. I'm just fucking reeling, okay?" She takes a pillow and holds it to her lap. "I don't know what to do. I don't even know what *lesson* I'm supposed to learn." She wipes some wetness from her eye. "Maybe I'm not corrupt enough to be successful. I mean, is this what happens? Is this what we do? Create these dramas for ourselves? All the shit that's going on in Sudan or Cape Breton and here we are creating our own little drama in Toronto? In the amount of time allotted to us? On this place called Earth? Because there's *got* to be more to life than the circle of people we fuck and do business with. Small world? Not really. We have small lives but the world out there is big, big, big." She bites her lip. "And I hate all of it."

"Let's get out of this hotel room," Brendan says gently. "We'll blow off the gala. I'll take you out for dinner." He bends down and kisses the top of her head.

At this touch, Hannah's hand shoots into the air, fingers splayed. "Just don't *fuck* with me right now," she says. "Go have your shower. I'll be fine. Really." She makes a quick, mechanical smile then looks at the floor, silent as Brendan walks into the bathroom.

A few minutes after the shower starts, Hannah rises from the bed and shoves the curtains open. The sky is clear.

She looks from its blueness to the street below. She watches as two women hurry across the street, both wearing red pants. "No one in this city knows how to dress," she says.

Behind her, the fallen cell phone begins ringing on the carpet. Hannah retrieves it. "Hello?" she says. "Errol! Didn't Brendan get back to you? I'm so sorry." To support herself, she puts her other hand on the dresser. "What am I *wearing?* Errol, you sure you have the right number?" She shifts her weight from one leg to another. "Oh, you mean to the gala. What am I wearing tonight?" She listens a moment then bends forward with musical laughter. "Oh, Errol, my virgin ears! Well, you know me." Her voice slips into a lower, more intimate register. "Love galas. *Love* galas. But actually, doll, I'm not sure about tonight. I have some reading to do." She glances down at the manuscript. "A friend's book, actually. A memoir. But I don't think it's your thing, Errol. It's too sexy for you."

As the sounds of the shower begin to end, Hannah walks to the bathroom door and closes it. "You like the big wham-o stuff with explosions and superheroes. This is quite a nice piece. A love story. I don't think it's your thing at all. Why?" She listens again, her fingers playing with the hem of her slip. "To be honest, it's not that good a book but it might make a brilliant fucking movie. Because the story it *wants* to be?" She turns to look into the blue sky. "I want to make that movie. For sure I'd want to make that movie. Who wouldn't?"

Shimmer

IT'S THE BIGGEST Deedee party ever. Walking up to the house, Sheri and Celeste can't believe how many people they don't know. Some people they recognize, like the stoner kids who hang around the school parking lot, and those jocky guys, and the girls doing cartwheels in the snow Celeste remembers from gymnastics. But those guys by the cars – aren't those the guys from Shop? And is that like a basketball team from a whole other high school? And those punk rock guys with green hair staring at them – whose friends are they? Look at them, unloading guitars and stuff from a van, what school are they from? How does Deedee even *know* them?

I can't breathe, says Celeste, shivering. There's too many people.

Can you believe this? Sheri says. There's like two hundred people here already. I hope Deedee's parents really went to Florida.

Fuck. My mom wants me home by eleven tonight.

Like that'll happen.

Maybe I won't go home tonight, says Celeste. Maybe I'll just kill myself first.

I hate that joke.

I'm serious.

Yeah well who isn't, Celeste?

I'll probably commit suicide around midnight. In case you can't find me.

Then can I keep your black sweater?

No, I want it back.

Too bad, says Sheri. You'll be dead.

You have to give it back to my mother. And make sure you wash it so it doesn't smell like cigarettes.

As if your mom doesn't know you smoke. Fuck. Some people actually *do* commit suicide, Celeste, you freak.

INSIDE, it's more crowded. In the basement Sheri and Celeste walk by some people doing hot knives with a blowtorch. There's kids smoking dope by the freezer. Upstairs in the kitchen there's twenty cases of beer. Everyone's drinking beer. Want a beer? Celeste takes a beer from a guy she knows, Donny, he has a car, how old's he? Like nineteen. She pushes her thumb against the curve of the bottle but she doesn't feel like drinking. Who are all those people in the backyard? Through the kitchen window, Celeste sees twenty more people she doesn't know. The backyard goes right into the woods and it seems like people fade away into trees like they're at a bonfire. This is so crazy. Fuck, though. What should she do? It's the biggest party of the year and already she's feeling anti-social and not that drunk anymore. She sips the beer. It tastes weird. She doesn't really feel like drinking. Oh great she's going to be the only person to have a shitty time at the biggest party of the year.

You all right? Sheri asks, unzipping her parka.

Yeah it's just freaking me out how many people I don't know.

What a weird night, says Sheri. It was cold and now it's muggy.

Sheri!

What?

I told you not to say that word.

What word – muggy? Why?

It's like when people say nuggets. My mother says it all the time. It's disgusting. It makes me feel like I'm throwing up in my head.

Muggy nuggets, says Sheri. Muggy nuggets.

I'm serious, says Celeste, swatting at Sheri's beer. Fuck off. I won't be your friend anymore. You'll never borrow my clothes again.

What're you doing? Sheri slaps at Celeste's hand. That's my beer! Steal my grave that fast?

The front door opens and two people in ski jackets come in.

My God, says Sheri. It's Owen and Rowan.

The student *council's* here?

Owen and Rowan, says Sheri. Rowan and Owen. I'm so sick of hearing about Owen and Rowan. Everybody's favourite fucking couple. Who cares anyway? Why should we cow-tail to them?

Celeste lights a cigarette and gazes at them. How long they been going out?

Five years, says Sheri. Since grade six. Think they'll get married?

Celeste blows a smoke ring. I hope their baby's retarded.

She's so fake, says Sheri, frowning. I can't think of a faker, prissier, more stuck-up person. I'm glad she's short.

You should see her mother, says Celeste. She's like four foot nothing. She's a total midget. She's a shrimp.

Who's Rowan talking to?

Celeste recognizes the other girl. She was one of the girls doing cartwheels outside in the snow. That's that girl Angela Silver.

Who is she? Why does she have blue hair?

She's that stupid little bitch that got me kicked out of gymnastics.

How old is she?

Grade nine.

Didn't you used to hang around her all the time?

When I was in elementary.

How'd she get you kicked out of gymnastics?

I missed three practices and I said I was sick and she

told them I was lying. But Celeste looks down, remembering something else, something someone said Angela Silver said – that when Celeste got tits she stopped being everybody's friend and became some big slut. Yeah meanwhile Angela Silver's probably still a virgin with all her teeny-bopper friends still playing dress-up and tea party in the attic and they're how old? Fourteen, fifteen? And now she's dressing like a punk rocker? Give me a break Angela Silver's a punk rocker. Excuse me while I barf she's a punk rocker.

She looks like a little skank tonight, Sheri says, noticing the girl's blue hair, black nail polish, the safety pins in her jeans. Whatever. I'm going to go find Deedee.

Sheri starts up the stairs then comes back to grab her beer. And try not to be too much of a klepto, okay, Celeste? You big freak.

CELESTE LOCKS HERSELF in an empty bathroom and looks at herself in the mirror. She doesn't look that drunk. She takes a breath, pulls at her bangs, checks her eyeshadow, then turns to see what her ass looks like in these jeans. Facing front, she undoes a blouse button. The best tits in grade eleven, that's what Robby Delano said. And those other guys said she and Alison Andrews were the hottest girls in school. So with all these people here, there must be *some* cute guy she can flirt with. She should just turn on her fake personality and mingle and see how many guys she can get to like her. That used to be fun. Just the moment before, wondering if she can get them to make out with her, she loved that. That used to be everything.

Someone's knocking on the door.

Just a minute. Fuck! Celeste opens the mirror and looks in the medicine cabinet. Little bottles of Valium and Aspirin, Handi Wipes, a yellow hair elastic, Q-tips, a vacation photograph. Celeste snatches it. It's a photo of Deedee in front of the Grand Canyon. She remembers when Deedee came back from there. The most unbelievable place you ever saw, Deedee said. She couldn't even describe it. No one could explain it till they were there in person. All this nature. Looking at the photograph, Celeste wonders if she'll ever see it before she dies.

Someone knocks again.

Okay, okay, says Celeste. She grabs the Valiums and the Aspirins from the medicine cabinet and stuffs them in the front pocket of her jeans. Opening the door, she sees one of the punk rock guys, the guy with green hair. Is he ever tall – who is this guy? He kind of blushes and goes by so she smiles but it's too late, he's gone.

IN THE HALL, Sheri's talking with a bunch of people. There's some grade nine kid, somebody's lurpy little brother – that's Darren Myer's little brother – and some girl hanging off Sheri, barely standing up, she doesn't even know where she is. Fuck, that's Angela Silver.

Celeste walks over. What's going on? What are you doing with her?

Sheri shoves Darren Myer's little brother. Get the fuck away from her, you horndog asshole! Can't you see she's intoxicated? Can't you see she's practically passed out?

What'd she drink? Celeste looks at Angela Silver.

That guy made her drink it.

What was it?

I don't know. Sheri grabs a bottle off the carpet and reads the label. Bacardi. She chugged it. She chugged a pint of Bacardi.

Sheri and Celeste help Angela Silver downstairs to a bedroom and lay her on a bed. Celeste is taking off the girl's sneakers when Angela Silver lurches forward and throws up.

Fuck! Celeste jerks back. She puked on me!

Sheri finds two towels and a face cloth in the laundry room. She puts the towels over the puke then sits on the bed and wipes Angela Silver's mouth with the face cloth.

How you doing, Puke Face? You all right? Sheri looks up at Celeste. She should probably eat some bread or something.

Why? Standing beside the bed, Celeste checks her shirt for puke stains.

And someone should probably call her mother.

And what, Sheri – get the party shut down?

She might have to get her stomach pumped, all right? She could die from alcohol poisoning, you know, Celeste. And we'd be responsible.

Like I'm going to go to jail over a fourteen-year-old.

Remember Crystal-Ann Hobday? asks Sheri. She almost died in a snowbank. Think about it. She passed out in a snowbank after she had sexual intercourse with her own father! You think everything's a joke, Celeste, but it's not funny.

Sheri gets up, leaving the face cloth hanging from Angela Silver's nose. I'm going to find Deedee, she says, running up the stairs.

Celeste watches Angela Silver cough a few times. Hey Puke Face, how you doing? You going to puke again?

But Angela Silver is hardly conscious. She lies on her side, her eyes slow, her skin pale. There's puke on her shirt, one sneaker off, one sneaker lost. Celeste sits beside her on the bed. She smooths Angela Silver's blue hair away from her face and studies Angela Silver's jeans. The seams are spangled with safety pins and written on the denim in red ballpoint are names of bands Celeste doesn't know. She finds a Keds sneaker with black-and-white checkers drawn on it with black marker. Inside is a wrinkled pink sock. Celeste squints at it. Seeing the pink sock makes her remember something she doesn't want to remember. It makes her feel sick in her head like when Sheri said muggy. She's thinking about that when Angela Silver starts petting Celeste's knee with her fingers. What the fuck? Celeste stands up, disgusted. Jesus. She spits a mouthful of beer on Angela Silver. Go fuck your mother, punker, she says, leaving Angela Silver alone on the bed, burping, murmuring, not knowing where she is.

IN THE BACKYARD the sky's clear all the clouds are gone and it's cold again – what a weird night, it keeps changing – and Celeste finds Veeper staring at the stars.

Quite the bedhead there, Veeper, she says. What're you looking at?

Meteor shower, says Veeper. Always at the end of February. Because the Earth passes through an asteroid belt. Probably one of the asteroids will crash down here just like the one in Siberia that wiped out all the dinosaurs.

God is he stoned. She's never seen Veeper this stoned. Hey, says Celeste, pulling on his sleeve. Where's Wendell?

Fuck knows. But don't quote me on that.

It's me – Celeste – over here.

Veeper doesn't say anything for a second. Hey Celeste Over There, he says, looking at her now. His hair's kind of greasy so he's not as cute as he is normally but his eyes are smiling. Celeste loves Veeper. She doesn't really know what he thinks about – his mind is so everywhere and embarrassed – that's why he's shy with girls. She remembers back in elementary when Veeper had really long hair like a girl, she used to follow him around when she was so bored she'd do anything. She'd love to blow his mind one day and fuck his brains out.

How many T-shirts you wearing tonight, Veep?

Three.

Only three? What's wrong? Aren't you the guy that wears four shirts to school?

He pulls at a shirt. That was the old Veeper, he says.

I'm the new Veeper now. But don't quote me on that. He looks again at the sky. In Physics we learned the light from those stars left when the Cro-Magnons were inventing ketchup.

I'm so behind in Physics it's not funny, Celeste says. I don't have a clue.

But he's hardly listening to her. She can never say the right thing around him. Maybe he doesn't like her. Everybody's smart now. Oh well.

Yeah, Veeper you're definitely on your own wavelength tonight, Mister. What're you on?

This hash from Eddie Fong. I'm so fucking wasted. Veeper starts giggling and looks at his boots. Here we go, he says, taking a step. Walking in the snow. Walking in the snow. He closes his eyes. I'm so fucking wasted.

THERE YOU ARE, Sheri says. What're you doing out here?

Hiding, says Celeste. Talking about dinosaurs.

What'd you say to Veeper?

Secret boy talk. Later we're going to a mystery land of pink forests and purple rocks and green water.

Celeste! You're being weird again. I need you to be normal.

Why? Nothing ever happens and if it does it's going to happen to somebody else anyway so who cares?

Your boyfriend's here.

Fuck off – he is not! Celeste looks inside the windows of the house. She doesn't want to see her boyfriend. She doesn't want to deal with him and already she feels herself hating him. He's just so urgently gross, she says. I'm sorry but I'm going to fucking vomit if I ever see him again. She leans over and spits in the snow.

Sheri is staring at Celeste like she's crazy. Are you all right?

Yeah.

Then stop being such a freak, okay? You've been in a weird mood ever since we left my house.

Okay, Mom. Okay.

You want this beer? says Sheri. I can't finish it.

Celeste takes the beer and drinks from it.

You want me to go talk to him? Sheri asks.

Why didn't he call me to say he's coming out tonight?

I don't know, says Sheri. He's *your* boyfriend.

Celeste sighs, frustrated. God he's boring. He's the most boringest guy. Okay go talk to him. Tell him I want to break up.

Sheri is staring at her. Again? But you've only been back together a week!

FAR IN THE WOODS, Celeste runs away from the party. It's steep uphill past the backyard maybe rocks sticking up she has to be careful oh fuck so what if she cuts her jeans or a branch scratches her eye out or she falls and smashes her head on a stone. She runs faster and in her hand she has a forty-ouncer of Bombay Sapphire gin she stole from the freezer in the basement. Celeste watches her breath rise up in the cold air and into outer space and all the meteors. Finally she can breathe again just finally she can breathe. She takes the top off the gin and brings the bottle to her mouth. God she loves the smell of gin in winter, like perfume in air, she just loves the Jesus smell of it. Gin smells so beautiful because it smells like there's always more of it. And finally when she drinks she knows she doesn't have to be in the world anymore because she can just be in some weird cartoon land where everything goes and nothing's boring. She puts the bottle to her lips and swings it to the sky. Air bubbles up. Remember the first time she got drunk? At the parish dance, she split a jar of moose piss with Cathy Charles except Cathy didn't show up and Celeste drank all of it. Inside the gym she got so hot she had to go outside and barf. When the paddy wagon caught her she was directing traffic in the middle of the traffic lights. Is this your daughter? the police officer asked when he got her home. You little ten-dollar slut, her mother said. Thanks, Mom. Takes one to know one. Her own mother said that and now she remembers what she didn't want to remember before and wouldn't let herself remember before but it gets remembered anyway like a car flashing the wrong way down the street. She remembers when she was a little kid and her mother stayed out all night the first time. Remember that? Her mother coming home at seven in the morning, Celeste watching Saturday-morning cartoons and playing with her Polly Pocket when she finds her mom's panties in a shoe in the front porch, wrinkly pink panties with white elastic. Why would her mom leave her panties in her shoe? Where was she that she was taking off her fucking panties?

Celeste chugs from the gin bottle. It's quiet. The smell of skunk somewhere. She lets fresh darkness seep into the trees and feels for the pills in her jeans pocket. She could really do it this time. Why not? Who cares, whatever, fuck you, goodbye. Her body found the next day frozen in a snowbank like Crystal-Ann Hobday. Why is she always thinking this? But it's so easy. How could you *not* think it? Why wouldn't you want it all over and done? She takes out the pills and empties them into her hand. When it's like this, when it gets inside her head like this, it's like keeping her finger over a candle or slicing her thumb with a pocket knife, the slit on her thumb like a little mouth with no eyes. Fuck, why is she *thinking* this? She doesn't even know if she's thinking it. How can she tell if she's thinking it? It's dominizing her thoughts. Dominizing? Is that a word? Celeste laughs loudly, drunk again, thank God, and feels she has to pee. She stuffs the pills in her pocket, pulls down her jeans and underwear, and squats down, her pee whizzing and steaming in the cold pine needles, into the ground, like when she peed in the middle of the street at some slumber party. Celeste remembers watching her own pee stream down the pavement and gather in a puddle at the bottom of the street. Someone dared her to do it. Angela Silver or somebody. When was that? Summer of grade six. Playing hide-and-seek with Angela Silver and her friends. God, that was fun, all those rich kids in that nice neighbourhood, hiding under the train bridge, making up songs, chewing that gum, what was that peppermint gum, the gum with the liquid centre? You can't get that anymore. Freshen-up gum, she remembers as a snowball explodes against a tree.

Who's that? Celeste stands and pulls up her clothes, her underwear twisting in her jeans. Who the fuck is that?

She hears a kid running in the woods.

Fuck off you little maggot, she says, striding away, untwisting her underwear and fastening her jeans. She doesn't notice when the pills, the pills she stole from the bathroom, spill from her pocket and disappear in the grey of a snowdrift.

CELESTE SITS DRUNK outside with the stoners, cross-legged by the woodpile, burning a hole through a leaf with a cigarette. But it's so cold her fingers are numb and she can't make the hole perfect. Three of the stoners throw lit matches at each other and they fizz and bounce on the frozen snow beside her. A match flames by her head, pffts, goes out.

Fuck off you little pyros, Celeste says. You could have blinded me! Do that again and I'll smack you, douchebag.

Go douche yourself, a kid says.

And I find out who the little dinkweed was that threw the snowball at me, you're dead. I mean if you're going to throw something at me, at least do it to my face.

Inside the house, someone starts playing an electric guitar. Everybody looks up. Celeste watches the punk rockers jump up and down in the living room. That tall guy with green hair is screaming into a microphone, green bangs caught in his eyelashes. It makes Celeste want to go in there and flip them out of his eyes. Another guy gets pushed into a drum kit. So why is everyone into punk rock now? Like skater kids and flumpy girls in drama, okay, but normal people like Angela Silver? And don't punks hate everything? Why are they so mad? They're mad at stuff they do anyway like posing and being pretentious. It doesn't make sense. Why do they get to be so mad?

Sheri stumbles by with somebody – she's got her arm around somebody – it's that lurpy little guy, Darren Myer's little brother. Oh my God Sheri's getting together with a grade nine?

Celeste grabs Sheri's foot. Hey there you freak. How you doing? You all right?

Fuck, you scared me! Where were you?

Doesn't matter.

What were you doing?

Something else that doesn't matter.

Sheri turns to Darren Myer's little brother. This is my friend Muggy.

Hi Muggy.

Hey.

So Celeste, what time's it? What time you staying till?

I'm going soon. It's like one-thirty.

You're going? You need to stay at my house?

Celeste looks at Darren Myer's little brother then smiles at Sheri. Don't worry about it, she says. I'll just act normal and go home. It's okay. I'm probably not that drunk. Did you talk to my dumb boyfriend? What'd he say?

Sheri wipes some hair off her face. He thinks you hate him. He thinks you hate him so he's being like "Oh she hates me so I don't like her first" type thing. I said "Celeste doesn't hate you."

It's such a fucking diddly-bop thing. Did you tell him I want to break up?

No. Because I know you don't mean it. But Celeste he's going to try and get everyone against you, I can tell.

I don't care. Let him go play his fucked-up little games. He's got mental problems. Trying to make it so complicated. It's not complicated. It's obvious. *He's* obvious. Fuck. Celeste stands up. I'm going.

Wait for us, says Sheri. I'm just going to say goodbye to Deedee.

For a second, Celeste watches Sheri walk off with Darren Myer's little brother. Behind her, in the woodpile there's a bug, a silverfish, frozen in a crack.

FROM THE BACKYARD, Celeste walks between the houses toward the street. This is obviously the worst night of anyone's life so she'll just walk home like a loser. Who cares at this point? Maybe she'll break up with her boyfriend for real this time. She can get another boyfriend and tell the old one to fuck off but it won't matter. Nothing really ever matters. She makes herself take a big breath because she feels like she's about to cry. She feels like she's about to cry for no reason so she looks up at the sky, watching for the glow of the meteor shower, wondering if Veeper is still here. Veeper at least listens to people. What did he say? Here we go, walking in the snow. God that was cute. Just the way he said it. Like a little kid.

Celeste clears a tear from her eye and between the houses a bird swoops past, a sparrow or swallow and then she remembers the word starling. She's remembering the word starling when she hears someone crunching in the snow behind her and she turns to see that guy, the guy with green hair, the punk rock singer, looking at her, so she says, You got a staring problem?

Sorry.

Oh, she says. I thought you were somebody else.

Are you Celeste Tupp?

Are you a police officer?

Huh? No.

Then yes I am. She smiles and he sort of blushes again. He's nice. This guy is actually nice. You can tell.

I was pretty sure it was you, he says. Because I saw you at a dance once with your friends. You were in a black sweater. I know it sounds stupid, but I always knew I'd see you again.

Doesn't sound stupid. What's your name?

Josh.

So you just decided to come out and say hi? Are you in that band? You don't exactly look like a punk rocker. Except your hair.

Those guys borrowed my amp. I just sang one song. I'm in another thing. Look, I didn't mean to bother you. If you're meeting your friends or something.

You didn't bother me, says Celeste. Hey look. She points at the window on the side of the house. My reflection in the window's talking to you.

He turns to see Celeste's reflection in the window.

Now she's smiling. Now she's laughing. Now she's gone. What's your name again?

It's still Josh.

You hear about the meteor shower?

Yeah. He looks into the sky. I haven't seen it yet.

Yeah, I should probably stay up and watch it. But I only got four hours sleep last night. I went to sleep at five and got up at nine. She yawns and lets her hair fall across her eyelashes, one of her eyes moist, her lips open.

I know you're probably going, Josh says, glancing at her. But I just wanted to say I think you're really great.

Celeste doesn't say anything. She puts her hand on the back of his neck and pulls him close to kiss him. He kisses her back, his teeth bumping hers, so she makes her mouth soft, matching her lips to his mouth. One of her hands moves to his waist. But what's he doing? She moves her head to one side.

What're you doing? Are you holding your breath?

I don't know where to breathe, he says.

You can breathe in your nose, she says, putting a hand on his cheek. Or breathe me. She kisses him again. Yeah. Just breathe me, she says. Breathe me.

MIX
Paper
FSC® C100212

Printed by Imprimerie Gauvin
Gatineau, Québec